ZACK

AUSTIN FUSION
BOOK 1

SAMANTHA LIND

SAMANTHALIND.COM

Zack
Austin Fusion Book 1
Copyright 2024 Samantha Lind
All rights reserved.
Print ISBN: 978-1-956970-40-1
Alternative Cover ISBN: 978-1-956970-41-8

No part of this book or cover have been created with the aide of AI technology.

No part of this publication may be reproduced, transmitted, downloaded, distributed, stored in or introduced into any information storage or retrieval system, in any form or by any means, whether electronic, photocopying, mechanical or otherwise, without express permission of the publisher, except by a reviewer who may quote brief passages for review purposes.

This book is a work of fiction. Names, characters, places, story lines and incidents are the product of the author's imagination or are used fictitiously. Any resemblances to actual persons, living or dead, events, locales or any events or occurrences are purely coincidental. Trademarked names appear throughout this novel. These names are used in an editorial fashion, with no intentional infringement of the trademark owner's trademark(s).

The following story contains adult language and sexual situations and is intended for adult readers.

Cover Design by Y'All That Graphic.
Cover image by FuriousFotog
Cover Model Chase Ketron
Editing by *Editing4Indies*
Proofreading by *Proof Before You Publish*

Created with Vellum

CONTENTS

Synopsis	1
1. Zack	5
2. Courtney	19
3. Zack	28
4. Courtney	38
5. Zack	51
6. Courtney	70
7. Zack	84
8. Courtney	101
9. Zack	108
10. Courtney	115
11. Zack	121
12. Courtney	132
13. Zack	144
14. Courtney	159
15. Zack	171
16. Courtney	187
17. Zack	196
18. Courtney	206
19. Zack	216
20. Courtney	227
Coming Soon	237
Also by Samantha Lind	239
Acknowledgments	241
About the Author	243

SYNOPSIS

ZACK

She's my best friends little sister
Completely off limits
I know I should resist her... but I can't
She's fresh out of a bad relationship
And five years younger than me.

But there is this invisible string that just pulls us together.

He's so far out of my league,
But that doesn't change the fact I can't get him out of my mind
Or my dreams
Or my bed

I gave love a chance and it burned me badly.
His promises are enticing, but is it worth giving love a second chance?

DEDICATION

To all my OG readers....This one is for you! Cheers to sticking around all this time, and to book number 30!

1

ZACK

I sit on a stool overlooking the rink below me, watching as the puck slides along the slick surface and four kids chase it into the corner.

"That's it, Sawyer. Dig it out," I mutter as I watch my son dig at the puck trapped along the boards. He taps it out to his teammate, who skates it back along the net before centering the puck right back onto Sawyer's stick as he flips it over the goalie's pads and into the back of the net.

I put two fingers between my lips and whistle as the entire parent section goes wild for the goal. "That's how you do it, buddy!" I yell out. After fist-bumping his teammates, Sawyer looks up to where I like to sit when I can make it to his game and flashes me a smirk. The little shit sometimes gets a big ego when he makes plays like that happen. Guess the apple doesn't fall far from the tree.

"Hi, Zack." The most annoying voice filters into my space. I look over and see one of the moms of Sawyer's teammates.

"Brandy," I greet, trying to hide my disdain for this woman.

"Good to see you made it to a game," she says, and I can't miss her dig at the fact that I miss a lot of Sawyer's games. It just comes with the territory of my job.

"I don't miss them just because. It's kind of hard to be here when I'm in another state or country. Was there something you needed?" I ask, hoping to encourage her to leave me alone.

"We're collecting donations for the raffle basket fundraiser for the tournament next month, and I wanted to see if you could donate something to the cause."

"Of course. I'm sure Emerson is already putting something together for Sawyer's contribution, so she'll let me know what she needs from me."

I don't miss the eye roll from Brandy when I mention my ex. I'll have to ask Emerson about that when I talk to her after the game. "Oh, that makes sense. We'll always accept extra donations, so don't feel like you can't do your own, if you'd like."

I give her a little grunt, letting her know I heard

what she said, but my attention is drawn back to the ice, where the refs have just awarded Sawyer a penalty shot after being taken down on a breakaway. He stands at center ice, waiting for the signal from the ref that he can start. He circles around behind the puck before tapping it forward. *Keep your head up,* I mentally tell him as he skates down the ice. The goalie comes out to the top of his crease as he takes in Sawyer's moves. He skates the puck out to his left, then cuts back in toward the net just below the faceoff circles. The goalie flops forward and attempts to poke check the puck off Sawyer's stick but misses, leaving his net wide open. Sawyer skates around the goalie and dumps the puck into the back of the net. The goal horn blares as the bench and crowd all go crazy for his second goal of the period. He once again looks up at me for a nod of approval. I can't hide the smile on my face with how proud of him I am.

"Great game, kiddo." I rub the top of Sawyer's sweaty head once he comes out of the locker room with his hockey bag slung over his shoulder.

"My stats are almost as good as yours." He smiles up at me.

"Something like that." I chuckle. "Maybe you'll pass me up on the stat sheet one day."

"Can we get burgers for dinner tonight?" he asks as we make our way out of the hallway.

"I don't see why not. But before we leave, let's go talk to your mom," I tell him as we maneuver our way through all the parents waiting for their kids.

"Mom!" Sawyer calls out as he drops his bag and jogs over to where she's talking to other parents.

"Hey, kiddo, great game today."

"Thanks, I got player of the game," he tells her as he holds up the team necklace passed around after each game.

"Well deserved. I'll add another tally to your hat trick list," she tells him. "Hey, Zack," Emerson greets.

"Hey, Brandy cornered me about some basket donation. Do you need anything from me for that?"

"Can you do a signed T-shirt and a few pucks?"

"Shouldn't be an issue. Do you want a four-pack of tickets to a future game? I'm sure I have some vouchers I can donate."

"That'd be awesome. I can put together a second basket for a night at a game."

"Cool. I'll ask the office if there's anything else they can toss in and let you know."

"What are you boys up to tonight?" she asks as she slings an arm around our son.

"Apparently, we're doing burgers for dinner. Otherwise, no plans," I tell her. "Do you need me to drop him off by a specific time tomorrow?" One thing Emerson and I have done right is learn how to co-parent well.

We get along, and we make sure that Sawyer is always number one. Being a professional hockey player means my schedule is all over the place for more than half of the year. Emerson and I couldn't make it work as a couple, but we didn't let that get in the way of parenting our son.

"I'd say no later than eight so he can get to bed on time for school Monday morning, but otherwise, nothing major is going on tomorrow. If you could just text me so I know if I'll need to plan on him for dinner."

"Sounds good. We'll decide what to do, and I'll keep you in the loop," I say.

"Have a good night. Love you, buddy," she tells him before kissing his cheek. The tips of his ears turn pink. He's probably embarrassed his mom just kissed him in front of his friends.

I smack the back of his head with a love tap. "Don't roll your eyes at your mom," I tell him. "That's disrespectful."

"Sorry, ma'am," he apologizes and kisses her cheek as a bonus.

"You're forgiven. Love you, and I'll see you tomorrow sometime."

I snag Sawyer's bag and sling it over my shoulder. "Do you want to go out for burgers or stop at the store and grab stuff to grill at home?" I ask as we make it out to the parking lot.

"Burgers!" he exclaims. "Can we go to that one place with the video game room?"

"I suppose," I tell him as we walk out to my truck.

During the entire drive to the restaurant, he fills me in on his past week at school and practice. If my kid isn't missing one thing, it's that he has a way with his words. He's full of life, and I wouldn't change that for anything.

"Hi, a table for two, please," I say to the young girl at the hostess stand.

"It will be just a second. I have someone wiping down tables."

"No problem," I tell her as we step aside and wait. It doesn't take long before we're being led back to a booth and handed menus.

"Our special today is the double bacon cheeseburger with fries and a shake of your choice."

"Can I get that, Dad?" Sawyer pipes up almost immediately.

"If that's what you want, then sure," I say. "It's going to be big with two patties."

"I'm a growing boy. I eat a lot," he says, and the attitude rolling off him makes me chuckle.

"Is that so?" I raise an eyebrow in question.

"That's what Mom tells me. She says I'm going to eat her out of house and home, whatever that means."

I can't hold back the laugh at Sawyer impersonating Emerson. I can see her saying something like that, and he nailed the impression of her doing so.

"Guess I might have to up the amount of money I send your mom each month to help cover your food bill," I tease.

"Hello, I'm Courtney, and I'll be taking care of you today," says the sweetest voice I've heard in a long-ass time, pulling my attention from the menu.

"Courtney." I say her name as I take her in.

"Holy crap. Zack, is that you?" she asks as I slide out of the booth to pull her into a hug. I had no idea my best friend's little sister was back in town or, better yet, working here at this burger joint.

"The one and only," I confirm. "What are you doing here? I didn't realize you were back in town."

She blows out a breath, the hairs around her face fluttering as she does. "I haven't been back long, just a few weeks, actually. Picked up a second job here on the weekends to help pay the bills."

"What's dickwheezle doing?" I ask, my disdain for her baby daddy not in check.

Courtney laughs at my name for him. "Chad and I broke up. He stayed back in Houston, which is for the best," she says, and I can tell there's more to that story. "I packed up Jax and we moved back to be around family. Got us a little apartment, and I'm back on my own two feet."

"You should have called. I'd have helped," I say.

"I needed to do this on my own. I didn't even accept much help from Ryan. I moved in with Mom and Dad for a couple of weeks until I could find a place to rent and get a paycheck in the bank."

"I'm here. If you need anything, just call." I give her a hard stare so she knows I'm serious.

"Thanks," she finally concedes. "What can I get the two of you to eat and drink?" She changes the subject as she pulls out her order pad.

"We'd both like the special. I'll take a chocolate shake, and Sawyer will take a..." I look at him across from me to answer.

"Chocolate with sprinkles, please," he says, and I can't help but beam at him for remembering his manners.

"Of course. Do you both want whipped cream on top?" Courtney asks.

"Yes, please," Sawyer answers. My mind drops immediately to the fucking gutter, thinking about whipped cream and Courtney. *Where the fuck did that come from?*

I clear my throat and the picture from my mind. "Sure," I say.

"Alright, I have two double bacon cheeseburgers with fries and two shakes coming right up. Can I get you anything else? Maybe a couple glasses of water?"

"That'd be great," I state, giving her a half smile.

"Can we go play games while we wait?" Sawyer asks as Courtney walks away. My eyes follow her as she goes. The sway of her hips has me hypnotized. "Dad," Sawyer says again, waving a hand in front of my face.

"Games, yes," I say as I slide out of the booth. I reach into my back pocket and pull out my wallet, fishing out a twenty to hand over to Sawyer. I watch as he feeds the cash into the machine that then spits out a card with the credits for the games. He races over to a two-player racing game and swipes the card. The game lights up with a screen instructing us to select our race car. We each pick one out, and the video screen flashes to the racetrack. "You ready to eat dust?" I joke.

"You're the one going to be eating dust." He smirks.

"We'll see about that," I say as numbers flash down from three on the screen. As soon as it flashes GO, I press the gas pedal as hard as I can, and my car takes off. Video game cars aren't as easy to control as my own, so I fishtail all over the place as Sawyer leaves me in his dust. The way he cackles with laughter from his seat has me even more determined to beat him.

I finally gain control of my car and start gaining speed on the other cars in the race. The numbers in the corner tell me what place I'm currently in, and I've successfully made it into third place. Only one computer-controlled car and Sawyer's stand between me and first place. "I'm catching up. You better not crash," I trash-talk.

"Not happening, old man." He gives it right back to me. He makes some fancy move and then stands with his hands in the air, celebrating that he crossed the finish line in first place. "That's right! That's how you do it." He hops around all excited. I ended up in second place, but all he cares about is the fact that he won.

"Alright, what are we playing next?" I look around at our options.

He does the same. "How about Skee-Ball?"

"Now, that I can do," I say as I confidently walk over to the wall lined with the machines. He swipes the card for two of them, and the balls come sliding down the shoot.

"May the best man win." I smirk as I pick up my first ball and send it flying up the ramp. It expertly flies off the lip and lands dead center in the hardest-to-get hole at the top—100 points ding on my machine.

"Dad," Sawyer whines as his ball bounces off one of the sections and rolls down, only getting him ten points.

"No whining, no complaining," I remind him. "Try again, and see what you can get." I grab my next ball. This one isn't as successful as the first and gets me just ten points. Sawyer lands his second one in the circle

ZACK

for fifty points, which perks him up some as we go back and forth, taking turns to see who will win. After I throw my final ball, my score is 240.

"Think I can beat you?" Sawyer asks as he tosses his final ball up in the air slightly like it's a baseball. I look at his score of 220.

"Maybe, and there's only one way to find out," I say, nodding my head in the direction of his machine. He squares his body up, focusing hard on the targets as he winds his arm back and sends the little white ball sliding up the ramp. It hops off the ledge and has a nice little arc to the jump. It hits the edge of one of the circles and plops down into it—twenty points. We've tied! "Nice shot." I rub the top of his head, messing up his hair. "Way to tie your old man." I pull him into me, hugging him.

"Zack, your food is ready," Courtney says as she steps up next to us.

"Perfect timing. Thanks for letting us know." I smile down at her and don't miss the way her cheeks tint pink when I do.

"Let's eat while our food is hot," I suggest to Sawyer. "Then we can come play some more."

"I'm starving!" he announces, and both Courtney and I can't help but laugh at his antics as he runs back to the table where our food has been placed. He licks a

15

big glob of whipped cream off the top of his shake. "Mhmm, this is amazing."

I take a seat in the booth. "Is there anything else I can get either of you right now?" Courtney offers. *You in my bed.* The unbidden thought pops into my head, but I bite my tongue to keep from actually saying it.

"I think we're good, thanks," I manage to say without sounding like something is wrong. Not that my cock swelling in my pants is bad. It's just not the best time or place for that appendage to come to life.

"I'll let the two of you be and check back in a bit," Courtney says before stepping away and stopping at another table.

"Can we go to the hockey store before we go home?" Sawyer asks.

"What do you need there?" I ask.

"Tommy has a new stick that is sick. I want one," he says.

I can't help but chuckle at that. "What's wrong with the sticks you already have?" I quirk an eyebrow at him.

"But, Dad, it was so cool. It has a different grip, and the colors match our jerseys." He's doing his best to sell me on this really hard.

"I'm sure it does, but that doesn't mean you need a new stick today. You have a handful of them already. You can't always get the newest releases just because they look cool."

"But Daaaaad." He drags out my name. *"You get new sticks all the time."*

"That's a little different. I'm paid to play hockey. I get them as part of my job and from my endorsement deals. Not just because I think they look cool on the showroom floor."

"Man," he complains.

"Put it on your birthday or Christmas list, or for when you grow again and need a longer stick."

"But we don't know when that will happen, and my birthday is so far away. Christmas, too."

"Sorry, buddy. You know the drill. We don't buy stuff the moment we learn about it just because."

We both go back to paying more attention to eating than talking. I'm a little shocked he eats as much of the large burger as he does. It was incredible and filling.

"I'm stuffed," I say, pushing my now empty plate away from me.

"Same," he says with about a third of his burger left and half of the huge portion of fries.

"Do you want to take your leftovers with us for later?" I ask.

"Sure." He shrugs his shoulders. I look around and see Courtney just finishing up with another table. As she steps away, I get her attention, motioning that we need a box.

A couple of minutes later, Courtney returns with a

box and our check. "How was everything?" she asks as she picks up my empty plate and stacks our empty shake cups on top.

"Amazing," I reply.

"The best ever!" Sawyer says.

"I'm glad." She laughs at his enthusiasm.

"Here, you can take this with you." I hand over the bill folder with my credit card tucked into it.

"I'll be right back." She smiles at me, and the gesture makes my heart do this little flutter. *Where the hell did that come from?*

I place Sawyer's leftovers into the to-go box while we wait for Courtney to return with my card and the receipt for me to sign. She does so quickly, and I sign it, leaving a hefty tip.

"It was great to see you. Don't be a stranger. If you and Jax want to come out for a game one night, let me know, and I can get you a set of my comp tickets."

"He'd love that. It was so great to see you. I'm glad the two of you came in tonight."

"See ya around." I give her a quick hug before heading out to my truck with Sawyer.

2

COURTNEY

Beep, beep, beep. The blaring noise from my alarm wakes me from a dead sleep. It's way too early for the day to start, but that's my reality these days. I climb out of bed and walk over to my dresser, pressing the button to turn my alarm off. If I don't have it set across the room from me, I'll just reach over, shut it off, and go back to sleep.

With my alarm off, I raise my arms up over my head, stretching my tired body. Working the weekends at the Burger Shack puts me on my feet for hours at a time, and I'm just not used to that. Add in the forty hours a week I work at a day care, taking care of toddlers, and I'm one tired girl.

I slip on some workout clothes and head out to the small living room. I remain as quiet as possible so that Jax stays asleep while I get in my morning workout. I pull up the streaming app and flip through the classes, find a thirty-minute stretching one, and get settled.

Once finished, I head for the shower, and then it's on to getting dressed, waking Jax up, and feeding him breakfast before it's time for us to leave in the morning. Thankfully, he can come to work with me and catch his school bus from there.

"Hey, little man." I rub his back as he sleeps soundly in his bed. He's not much of a morning person, not that I blame him. He rolls over, rubbing at his face as he wakes up.

"Mornin', Momma," he groggily greets.

"Did you sleep well?" I ask as he sits up.

"Yeah." He yawns as he stretches.

"Ready for some breakfast?" Occasionally, he'll wait to eat breakfast until after we're at the day care.

"Can I have French toast sticks?" he asks.

"I think we still have some. Let me go check. You get dressed and go to the bathroom," I instruct him before leaving his room to check the freezer. I'm in luck because the box has five sticks left. I pop them into the toaster oven and immediately add them to the grocery list hanging on my fridge.

By the time the toaster oven timer dings, Jax has made his way to the table, where he's sitting nicely and waiting for his breakfast. I pour him a small cup of milk and add a small amount of syrup to his plate before setting everything down in front of him. I kiss the top of his head before I go back for my cup of coffee and bowl of yogurt and granola.

"What do you want for dinner tonight?" I ask as I sit down across from him to eat my breakfast.

I can see his mind at work as he thinks hard about the question.

"Spaghetti with meatballs and that really yummy bread," he says.

"The kind with the cheese?" I ask.

"Yep!"

"That's cheesy garlic bread," I tell him. "But spaghetti it is." I make a mental note to check that we have everything I'll need to make dinner. Otherwise, I'll have to stop at the store after work.

"Do I have to stay at school late again?" Jax asks after he finishes his food.

"Yes, that will be every day, now that I got you into the after-school program," I remind him.

"Why can't I just come with you?" he asks.

"I wish you could, but they don't have an opening for you in the afternoons." I do my best to explain to him, but kid ratios don't mean much to most kindergartners.

"Oh." He sighs loudly.

"It looked like you were having fun on Friday when I picked you up."

"Yeah, but I was tired of being at school for so long."

"I know, buddy. It does make for a long day, but I need a safe place for you to be while I'm at work. They had an opening, so we'll have to stick it out for now and make the best of it."

"Okay," he easily agrees. If I'm thankful for one thing, it's how easygoing he is.

"If you've finished eating, go brush your teeth, and then you can pick out your snack for the day. Hot lunch is grilled cheese with apple slices. Do you want that or for me to pack you something?" I ask.

"Hot lunch," he answers as he races to the bathroom. I quickly clean up our breakfast dishes and place them in the dishwasher before I pack my lunch for the day. Twenty minutes later, we're in the car and on our way to work.

I COLLAPSE ONTO JAX'S BED WHILE HE PICKS OUT the book he wants me to read before it's time to sleep; the day was long and tiring. A room full of two-year-olds is exhausting, to say the least.

"This one!" he finally says, holding it out to me as he climbs into bed. I take the book and flip it over, reading the title, *Froggy Goes to Camp*. Ah yes, a favorite of his, and one that I could probably recite from memory, thanks to all the times I've read it.

I read the final page, yawning through the last few pages. As I close the book, I'm usually met with pleas to read a second one or the same one again, but not tonight. I look down at Jax and find him sound asleep. He looks so dang peaceful. I know packing him up and moving back to my hometown was the best thing for us both, but I still have those small shreds of doubt that make me wonder if it really was the best thing for him. To move him away from his dad and what he knew as home.

"I love you, baby boy," I whisper before pressing a kiss to his cheek. He doesn't flinch a muscle at the contact, so I know he's already in a deep sleep for the night. I stay for a few more seconds, soaking in the moment with him before heading into the bathroom to get ready for bed. I'm just as exhausted as he is and ready to crawl into my own bed.

I wash my face and apply some night face cream before I head back into the kitchen and finish up the last few dishes that need to be hand washed from dinner. I packed up the leftovers to take for lunch tomorrow, so that's one less thing I'll have to do in the morning, which is always a win. Once my kitchen is clean, I snag the grocery list off the fridge and look it over, then check the fridge and pantry to make sure I didn't miss writing down anything we need. Once I'm confident my list is complete for the next week or so, I take it with me to bed. I pull out my tablet and sign in to the grocery store's website to submit my online order. I swear, online grocery shopping was the best invention, especially for busy moms who don't have time to shop. I check my online cart one last time before hitting the submit button and choosing my pickup window for after work tomorrow.

With that chore done, I pull up my book and read a few pages before sleep claims me.

Oh, Zack, yes, harder. Fuck me harder. I pant as he thrusts his cock into me. I have never been fucked this hard, nor have I ever had multiple orgasms during one session of sex. I'm just about to come when someone shakes me and calls Mom.

I bolt up, waking from the most vivid dream I've ever had. I can't believe I was dreaming about Zack and I having sex. My breathing is labored after that dream and being woken up suddenly.

"What's wrong?" I ask Jax. He's standing next to my bed, looking at me as I take him in.

"I puked," he says, tears sliding down his cheeks.

"Oh, buddy, where did you puke?" I ask, hoping and praying that it isn't in his bed.

"The bathroom floor. I couldn't make it to the toilet." He cries a little harder.

"Don't worry about it. I'll get it cleaned up. How's your tummy now?" I ask as I get out of bed.

"It hurts," he says.

"I'm sorry. Let's get you cleaned up and back to bed. Hopefully, one puke is all you needed."

"Okay, Momma."

I take him into my bathroom, stripping him down out of his pj's that have puke on them. "Do you want to take a shower or bath?" I ask.

"No, but can I sleep with you?" he asks.

"Of course." I pull him into a hug. "You go sit on my bed, and I'll grab you some clean clothes."

I get him dressed and tucked into the other side of my bed, then go into the main bathroom and clean up the floor. By the time I make it back to bed, he's sound asleep again. I check his forehead to make sure he isn't running a fever, and thankfully, he isn't. Hopefully, it was just something not sitting right in his stomach, as I can't afford to miss multiple days of work staying home with him. I check the time, and it's only two o'clock. I still have a few hours to sleep before my alarm goes off.

> COURTNEY
>
> Hey, any chance you're off today?

RYAN

I have some errands to run, but otherwise, I'm not busy today. What's up?

> COURTNEY
>
> Jax was up puking last night, so I can't send him to school. I really don't want to call in to work if I can avoid it. Any chance he can hang out with you today?

RYAN

Not a problem at all, Sis. Do you want me to come over there, or did you want to drop him by?

> COURTNEY
>
> I can bring him by. He says he feels better, so I think it was just dinner not settling right for some reason. We ate the same thing, and I've been fine.

RYAN

Not worried about some kid puke.

> COURTNEY
>
> You're the best big brother ever. I'll bring him over in about twenty minutes.

"Uncle Ryan said you can come hang out with him today."

"Yay!" he cheers, and I can absolutely tell he's back to his normal self. He just has to stay home from school due to the twenty-four-hour rule.

I run around, packing a bag for him for the day, grab my own, and we're out the door and on our way to my brother's house so I can drop Jax off before I head to work.

3

ZACK

"Hey, man, what are you up to today?" I ask Ryan once he answers his phone.

"Playing babysitter," he says.

"I'm not a baby." I hear a little boy's voice pipe up.

"Sorry about that. I'm kid sitting," Ryan corrects.

I chuckle at how quickly he changed his wording. "Who are you watching?" I ask.

"Jax for Court. He was up puking last night, and she didn't want to have to call off work, so I told her to bring him on by. I didn't have any clients booked for today, so it worked out perfectly," he tells me. Ryan is a personal trainer and sets his own schedule. "What are you up to?" he asks.

"Coach gave us today off. I went in for some treatment, but now I'm free. Want to grab some lunch?" I ask.

"Sure," he says.

"I can pick up something and come to you since you have Jax, if you want."

"That's perfect," he says, *"Hey, Jax, what do you want for lunch? My friend Zack is going to bring it over for us."*

I can't hear him reply, so I wait for Ryan to repeat his answer.

"He says chicken nuggets," Ryan says, *"but I'm not too keen on crappy fast food."*

"No problem, I'll swing in and grab him a Happy Meal and get us something else. I was kind of craving a chicken Caesar wrap."

"That sounds perfect," he agrees.

"I'll be there shortly," I say before disconnecting our call.

I tap on the contact for the restaurant I'm craving and place a pickup order. They tell me it will be about fifteen minutes, so I have plenty of time to swing through the drive-through and get the Happy Meal for Jax. When I arrive at the restaurant, my order is just being brought up to the pickup counter, so I quickly pay and am on my way to Ryan's place.

"Good to see you," Ryan greets me as I walk into his house. I set the food down on his kitchen island and start taking it all out of the bags.

"Good to see you, man. It's been too long." We slap

hands and pull each other into a man hug, smacking each other's backs in the process.

"Jax," Ryan calls out, and I hear little feet running down the hall toward us.

"Yes, Uncle Ryan," he answers.

"Lunch is here," he tells the little boy as he rounds the corner.

"Did you get me nuggets?" he asks, his curiosity evident.

"Sure did, little man," I tell him as I hold up the Happy Meal box.

"Yes!" he cheers, then moves to climb up on one of the barstools and bellies up to the bar.

I hold out my hand for him to give me a high-five, which he quickly does.

"What do you say to Zack for the Happy Meal?" Ryan asks.

"Thank you," Jax says as he tears open the box. He pulls out the box of nuggets, sleeve of fries, apple slices, and the toy.

"You're welcome. I wasn't sure what you wanted for the drink, so I got you some Sprite. Hope that's okay."

"Is that soda?" he asks. "My mom doesn't usually let me drink soda, only on special occasions."

"It is, but it doesn't have any caffeine, so hopefully, she won't be mad at me," I tell him.

ZACK

He digs into his food, hardly stopping as he inhales all of it.

Ryan and I both dig into our own take-out containers. The wrap I was craving hits the spot and fills me right on up.

"Want a beer?" Ryan offers once we've both finished eating.

"Nah, I'm good," I tell him. He pulls out a couple of bottles of water and motions to his patio.

"Want to chill outside?" he asks.

"Sure, I have nothing else going on. We might as well catch up."

We make our way out to the patio, and Jax follows us outside. He runs over to a deck box Ryan has on the edge and pulls out some toys.

"When did you get those?" I ask as I watch Jax play with a little kid's golf set.

"Just a few weeks ago when Court moved back home. I wanted to have some stuff here for when they visited, or for days like today. I might be a bachelor, but that doesn't mean I can't have stuff around for my nephew."

"Smart move," I say before taking a drink of the water he handed me. "I ran into Court the other day. Sawyer and I went to the Burger Shack after his game and sat at her table. It was good to see her again."

"I'm glad she moved back. Things were getting pretty bad from what she's told me," he says as he cracks his knuckles. I know my best friend well enough to know he isn't telling me the entire story, but I also know that the guy Courtney was with, Jax's dad, wasn't the greatest guy. Ryan never liked him. I might not have ever met the man, but Ryan's disdain for him is enough for me not to like him on principle.

"I hate that she's been through some shit. Hopefully, being back will be good for them."

"I can only hope," Ryan says as he looks out at his nephew. "She deserves to find someone who treats her like a princess. Shows her what real love is like."

I nod in agreement, my mind wandering to what I could show her. *Stop it, Blackburn. She's your best friend's little sister, not your next conquest.* I chide myself. "I hope she finds whatever she's looking for," I finally say.

"Hello?" Courtney calls out from inside the house.

"Out here," Ryan yells. I look over my shoulder and into the open sliding glass door. She's standing on the other side of the threshold, her hair in a messy bun, her T-shirt half untucked from her jeans. She looks tired and worn out from her long day at work, but her beauty still takes my breath away.

"Hey, how was he today?" she greets Ryan.

"He was great and has been playing hard all day. Ate his lunch and went right back to playing. Never would have known he was up puking in the middle of the night if you hadn't told me that."

"Good. I still have no idea what caused it, but I'm glad he's back to his normal happy self," she tells him before turning those beautiful blue eyes in my direction. "I didn't expect to see you here today. If I didn't know better, I'd think you were following me around," she teases.

"Coach gave us the day off, so I picked up lunch and came to hang out."

"I got to have Sprite with my lunch!" Jax tells Courtney as he runs up and wraps his arms around her.

"Did you now?" she says, giving Ryan a look.

"It wasn't me. Zack's the one who picked up lunch." He passes the blame to me.

"My fault. I didn't ask what he'd want before swinging through the drive-through, so I went with what I thought was a safe option with no caffeine."

"It's fine," she replies, a hint of amusement in her voice. "Thanks for getting him lunch. What do I owe you?"

"You don't owe me anything. I was happy to get him the Happy Meal," I say. I wouldn't take a dime of her money, even if it had cost me a hundred bucks.

"Are you sure?" she asks.

"Positive," I assure her, giving her what I hope is a *drop it* look. "How was your day at work?" I try to change the subject.

Courtney blows out a big breath before she plops down on one of the empty patio chairs. "Busy and long. Toddlers can be exhausting," she tells us.

"I've only had one, and I know how much he wore me out. I can't imagine a room full of them."

"Don't get me wrong, I love it, but damn, are they exhausting."

"Do you want to hang out and have dinner here?" Ryan asks Courtney, then his eyes flick to me.

"I don't want to impose," she replies.

"It isn't imposing when I'm the one asking if you want to stay." He chuckles.

"Then, yes, we'd love to stay," she says.

"Perfect, now, what do you feel like having?" he asks as he pulls out his phone. I'm guessing to open a delivery app.

"I'm not super picky," she says.

"Mexican? Chinese? Italian?" he asks as he scrolls on his phone.

"Tacos sound good. Especially if they have good queso and chips."

"Mexican it is. Are you staying?" Ryan asks.

"What the hell, tacos do sound good."

He taps at his phone, then hands it over to Courtney. "Order whatever you and Jax want, then pass it to Zack." She takes the phone and adds her order, then hands the phone to me. Our fingers touch slightly as we pass the phone, and a bolt of electricity shoots up my hand. By the way her eyes flash, she felt it, too.

"Everything good?" I ask as she quickly pulls her hand away.

"Yes," she replies, but it's a little breathy. I tuck that nugget of information away for later.

"Are we all set?" I ask as I read off everything in the cart. Ryan and Courtney agree, so I submit the order. "Looks like it will be here in thirty minutes."

"What's got you so distracted? Is something wrong?" Ryan asks Courtney.

I keep my eyes on her, taking in her stiff shoulders and slightly hung head. I didn't notice it until he said something, but something is definitely bothering her.

"I got a voicemail today from an attorney. Chad is filing for custody."

"That fucker!" Ryan seethes.

"I don't know what to do. I can't afford an attorney," Courtney says as a tear slips down her cheek.

"I have a good attorney. She helped Emerson and me with our custody agreement for Sawyer. I can give you her information."

"Thanks, but I'm sure I can't afford her rates," she says.

"Don't worry about the cost. Just call and talk to her," I tell her. I don't care what it costs. I'll pay every cent for her to keep her son.

"I can't let you pay for my attorney," Courtney argues.

"Then you can pay me back later." I shrug, knowing damn well I won't take a dime from her.

"Thanks, man. I appreciate you stepping in with your offer," Ryan says as he fist-bumps me.

"You're like family, and family takes care of one another," I state matter-of-factly.

"Mom, watch me!" Jax calls out, and pulls all of our attention his way. He stands behind the ball and concentrates before swinging the golf club. The plastic ball goes flying into the air, landing probably fifteen feet from where he hit it.

"Great job, buddy!" she calls out to him. "Keep practicing, and you'll be better than Uncle Ryan."

"I might have to take you to play mini-golf to check out your skills," Ryan tells him.

"Yes! Can we go tonight?" Jax asks.

Ryan chuckles. "Not tonight, buddy. I'm not sure what time they're open, and you have school tomorrow. But maybe this weekend."

"Yes!" he cheers, and goes to hit the ball once again.

4

COURTNEY

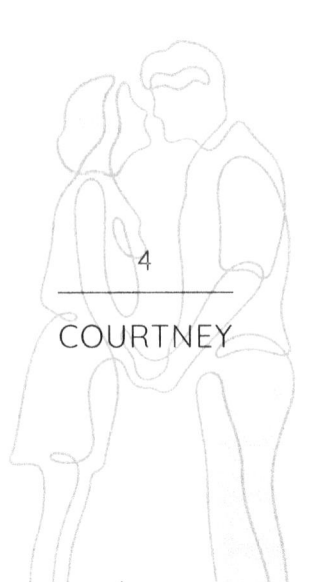

I sit at my brother's patio table. We have finished our dinner and are just conversing. My mind is still reeling over the message I received today from Chad's lawyer, and Zack's offer to use his attorney.

"Do you guys have plans this Saturday night?" Zack asks Ryan and me.

"I have a date," Ryan answers.

"Nothing that I know of, once I'm off work. Why, what's up?" I ask.

"Do you want to bring Jax to my game? I have ticket vouchers you could use," he offers.

"What time does the game start?"

"Seven, and usually they end around nine thirty or so."

"Jax, come here for a minute," I call out to my son.

ZACK

He sets down the golf club he's been playing with all evening and runs to the table we're all sitting at. "Yes, Mommy?" He looks up at me with all the love in the world.

"Zack has invited us to come watch his hockey game this weekend. Is that something you'd like to go do?" I ask.

"Can I play with you?" he turns to Zack and asks.

Zack chuckles. "Sorry, buddy, not this time. But maybe we can get you out on the ice sometime. This is my job, and you have to be on the team to play in this game."

"Oh," Jax says, a little defeated.

"You don't even know how to skate, buddy." I laugh. "I can't even think of a time we've tried to go ice-skating."

"Ice-skating?" he asks.

"Here, watch this," Zack offers, and holds out his phone. He presses play on the video, and a hockey game comes up.

"Is that you?" Jax asks in amazement.

"Yep, I'm in the blue jersey with the number 14 on my back," Zack tells him.

"Wow!" Jax says as the players zoom all over the ice in the clip. "What happened?" he asks.

Zack turns the phone to look at the video, then

turns it back so Jax can see. "I scored a goal," Zack tells him. "After we score, we all huddle together to celebrate, then go back to the bench to celebrate with the rest of our teammates."

"Can we go, Mommy?" Jax asks me, and I can tell he's excited about the idea of going.

"You're sure you have extra tickets? I don't want to impose."

"I wouldn't have offered if I didn't," he says.

"Okay, what time do you suggest we get there with it starting at seven?" I ask.

"Doors open around five thirty, but you don't need to be there that early. I have to go in around three thirty or four. Warm-ups start about six thirty. If you make it there by then, you can bring Jax down to the ice level and watch from the boards. I'll make sure to toss in the friends-and-family pass so you can get to the restricted area just for friends and family. Then, I can come say hi quick while we warm up."

"We should be able to make it by then, no problem. I get off work at three on Saturday," I tell Zack, then turn to Ryan. "If you want to meet me at the Burger Shack at three, I can just take Jax straight home. That way, you have extra time before your date."

"I can do that. Maybe I'll take him mini golfing before dropping him off to you," he says.

"That works for me, and I'm sure he'll love it."

ZACK

"I can drop off the ticket and passes tomorrow night, if that works for you. What time are you usually home from work?"

"Six thirty. Sometimes I get out a little bit earlier. It just depends on when the last kids in my room are picked up."

"Just shoot me a text when you get home, and I can swing by. Make sure to send your address, as well," Zack says. I don't know why the idea of him knowing where I live sends a bolt of lust down my body, but it does.

"Sure thing." Hopefully, my body isn't betraying me. Thoughts of my dream from this morning pop back in my mind, and I have to shake my head to get them out.

"You okay, Sis?" Ryan asks. "You're turning bright red."

"Just a little hot flash. I think my dinner was a little on the spicy side, and it's coming back to bite me." I try to blame the food.

Ryan gives me a skeptical look but doesn't say anything further. Thankfully, I can feel the heat leaving my cheeks, so hopefully, that means the redness is also disappearing.

"We need to head home in about ten minutes. Can you start picking up your toys, please?" I ask Jax.

"Okay," he quickly agrees and runs off and does as

asked. I lucked out with such a great kid. Not all moments are easy, but for the most part, things are easier now that we're no longer living with Chad. The saddest part of us moving back is he's only asked once about seeing Chad. Besides that one time, he hasn't shown any signs of missing his dad, so the idea that Chad is trying to get custody of him is just a knife to the heart.

Jax and I just got home from school and work. I have a roast in the crockpot, so dinner will be done soon.

"Why don't you put your backpack away, then wash your hands for dinner while I plate up our food," I suggest.

"Yes, ma'am," he says, and I think his little ma'am is so dang cute. He's picked it up at school, so other kids must be rubbing off on him.

As I'm plating our dinner, I remember I need to text Zack that we're home and my address. Once again, that jolt of lust for him hits me, and I do my best to push it away, thankful I don't have an audience this time.

COURTNEY

Hey, Jax and I are home. Just sitting down to eat some dinner. My address is 456 New Way Court, apartment 14.

ZACK

I'll head that way shortly. Did you have a good day? What about Jax?

COURTNEY

Good days all around. Just another long one. I'm tired and ready for bed.

I hit send before I think twice about talking about my bed with Zack.

ZACK

GPS says I'm about fifteen minutes away. Does that work, or do you want me to hold off for a little bit?

COURTNEY

That's fine. Drive safe, and I'll see you soon.

I set my phone down and take our plates to the little table. I go back for our glasses, filling Jax's up with milk and mine with lemonade from the fridge.

"Dinner's ready," I call out to Jax. I can hear the water running in the bathroom, so he must be washing up like I asked.

"Ready, Momma," he calls out as he comes down the hall.

"I hope you're hungry!" I tell him as I cut up the meat on his plate.

"Yep," he agrees as he climbs up on the chair. He grabs his fork and digs in. This is one of his favorite meals, so I always know it's a good choice.

We chat about his day. His class had library, so he tells me all about the book the librarian read to them before they got some time to check out books. "I brought home a new book to read tonight!" he excitedly tells me.

"What one?" I ask.

His eyebrows pull together as he thinks hard. "I don't remember the name," he says.

"That's okay. We can both be surprised when it's bedtime," I tell him as there's a knock on the door.

"Who's here?" he asks, looking over his shoulder toward the door.

"Zack is stopping by to bring us the hockey tickets to his game," I explain as I walk across the open floor space. I check the peephole to make sure it is Zack on the other side before I slide the lock and open the door.

"Hi," I greet him as he stands a good foot taller than me. "Come in." I step back and open the door all the way so Zack can step inside, and then close the door behind him.

"Smells good in here," he says, and waves to Jax.

"Are you hungry? We have plenty," I offer.

"I wouldn't want to impose," he says, and I toss his words right back at him.

"I wouldn't have offered if I didn't have extra." I smirk up at him as he realizes what just happened.

"Touché." He chuckles. "If you're sure, then yes, I'd love to stay and have some dinner."

I point at the table. "Go have a seat, and I'll be over with a plate for you. What can I get you to drink?"

"I'm good with just water."

I step into the kitchen and grab another plate. I add a large portion of pot roast, along with two scoops of the veggies and potatoes, then ladle out some extra gravy and pour that on top. I grab a clean glass out of the cupboard and fill it most of the way with water. I snag some silverware from the drawer before carrying everything over to the table and setting it down in front of Zack.

"Dang, this looks even better than it smells. Thanks again," he says before digging into the food. The moan that slips from his lips with his first bite is like a direct wire to my core.

"Like it?" I ask, already knowing the answer.

"Best meal I've had in a long time. You're a great cook," he compliments.

"I like to cook." I shrug. "But all I really did for this was dump it all in the crockpot and let it cook all day."

"It's my favorite!" Jax says.

"I can see why," Zack says. "How was school?"

"Good, we got to go to the library." He tells him the same story he's already told me.

I sit back and watch their interaction. They easily get along, and Zack actually sounds interested in what Jax has to say. Unlike when he'd try to tell Chad about his day or something that he was excited about. Don't get me wrong, I can only hear about superheroes or his favorite game so many times before I zone out, but even just talking about his day wasn't something Chad would do.

"Are you excited to come watch a hockey game?" Zack asks.

"Yes! Mommy let me watch videos last night. I like it when you hit the walls."

Zack chuckles. "So do most of the other people. If you come down by the ice for warm-ups, I can give you a puck to keep."

"Really?!" Jax's eyes light up.

"Yep," Zack tells him as he ruffles the top of his head, messing up his hair. "I should have brought you a jersey or shirt to wear. Maybe next time."

"That isn't necessary," I interject.

"Sure, it is. You've got to represent the home team." Zack winks at me, and I swear my stomach does summersaults because of it.

We continue to visit, keeping the conversation light

as we finish our food. Jax ended up with a second helping since he was so hungry.

"Go pick out your pajamas. It's almost bath time," I tell Jax.

"Okay. Can we still read my new library book?" he asks.

"Of course, we can," I say.

"Alright, well, I should get out of here and let the two of you get back to your normal routine. Once I'm at the rink on Saturday and changed out of my suit, I don't usually check my phone as it's in my locker. I put a sticky note in the envelope with one of the front office workers names and phone number. They can help you if you have any issues. There is a parking pass, the two game tickets, and the friends-and-family passes so you can come down by the ice. When you get inside the rink, just go to the VIP elevators and show them the passes. They'll direct you where to go," Zack explains.

"Thank you so much. I'm sure we'll figure it all out and enjoy watching you play," I say before I lean over and press a kiss to his cheek. I pull back immediately. I have no idea where showing that kind of affection came from, but my cheeks instantly heat in embarrassment.

"My pleasure," Zack says. His voice sounds husky, or am I just hearing things? The way he cups my cheek makes me realize I didn't hear things. "Have a good night, Court. I'll see you Saturday." He pushes back from the table and heads for the door. I watch as he opens it, but hesitates for a second, looking back at me before he pushes forward and walks out the door, pulling the door closed behind him. It opens just a second later, and Zack pops his head back in. "Make sure you lock up."

"I will." I get up and make my way over to the door. He closes it again, and as soon as I reach it, I flip the deadbolt.

"Good girl," he says through the door. That grumbly, deep voice does things to me, but I shake it off and go about my night, getting Jax ready for bed, reading his new book from school, and tucking him in.

Once he's asleep, I head for the kitchen and clean up from dinner. I pack up the leftovers into a few containers so I have lunch for work the next few days. Once the kitchen is clean, I check my menu on the fridge and pull out the chicken from the freezer, placing it in the fridge so it can start to defrost for tomorrow.

I shut off the lights and head into my bedroom. I'm tired but need a relaxing bath before I crawl into bed for some much-needed sleep.

I get the water to the right temp before closing the stopper so the tub fills. I add a scoop of my favorite lavender bath salts to the water. As I undress, Zack's words come back to me, and I can't help but think of him saying them in a bit more intimate situation and not through the door. I grab my iPad from my nightstand and my vibrator from the drawer where I have it hidden out of view.

I sink into the water, the heat instantly relaxing my tired muscles. I slide until I'm chin deep in the water, and rest my head back on the bath pillow. I take a few deep breaths, calming myself as the aromas of the salts take effect. After a few minutes of breathing, I tap on my iPad and pull up the Netflix app, but close it and open an incognito browser to search for porn. I can feel myself going red with embarrassment. I don't usually enjoy watching porn, but I'm desperate for a release. A popular website pops up, and I scan the page for something that looks like it might be enjoyable.

I finally decide on one, and my eyes go big when the screen fills with the video. Watching the guy on my screen go down on the girl has me imagining Zack as the guy and me as the woman, spread out on his bed. I grab my vibrator and click it on, then slip it beneath the water and down to my center. I slide it inside, the vibrations already causing my body to react from the simplest of touches. I click the button, and the clit portion comes to life and just about sends me over the edge as it flicks my clit.

I keep my eyes on the screen as I slide the vibrator

in and out of my pussy. I can feel myself clenching around the silicone, so I click the button again, increasing the vibrations, and that's all it takes for me to crest over the edge. I'm coming, and the only person on my mind is Zack.

5

ZACK

I shuffle back and forth as I stand in the locker room, waiting for the signal it's time to go. I'm nervous to hit the ice and see if Courtney and Jax made it to the game tonight. Sawyer couldn't come tonight, as he's out of town this weekend at a tournament. His team won their first two games and will play their next one while I'm on the ice playing my own. Thankfully, Emerson has kept me updated on their progress, and I was able to watch the livestream, as well.

"Let's fucking go!" one of my teammates calls out to the room at large. We're pumped and ready to take on Florida tonight.

Our starting goalie, Elijah Olson, raises his arm, his signal that he's headed down the tunnel and out onto the ice. We all fall into line, fist bumps handed out to one another and to the support staff as we pass by them. As soon as my skates hit the ice, my mind clicks over to warm-up mode. I take my normal two laps around our half of the ice before I collect a puck on the end of my stick. I look over at the friends-and-family section and see Jax and Courtney standing against the glass. A huge smile covers Jax's face and makes me smile just as big. I skate over to the glass and lean down to the small opening that the camera guys can open to take pictures and whatnot during the game.

"Hey, guys, glad you made it. I promised you one of these," I say to Jax as I pick up the puck and pass it through the small hole.

"A real puck!" he exclaims as he looks it over. It has a special logo on one side for tonight's game.

I laugh at his excitement. "A real puck," I confirm.

My eyes flash to Courtney's, and I find her smiling back at me. Her natural beauty hits me square in the chest like an arrow. "Have fun. I have to get to work."

"Be safe," she tells me before I skate away. I nod, letting her know I heard her. I join the line for warm-up drills, taking shots at the goal as we go through our routine.

"Who's the woman and kid?" Graham, one of our defensemen asks when I stop behind him.

"A family friend and her son. She just moved back to town, and her son has never been to a game, so I invited them tonight."

"Ah, you hitting that?" he asks.

I punch his shoulder, not that it does much with all the padding we wear. "Fuck off," I tell him as he takes off for his turn in the drill.

Once his line is done, I skate forward, waiting for the puck to be passed to me. It hits the end of my stick, and I send it flying to the net, beating Elijah on his blocker side.

"Lucky shot," he chirps as I skate by him. I chuckle at his cockiness and take my place in line once again.

"So was that a yes or no? She's pretty hot, so if you aren't hitting that, do you mind if I take a shot?" Graham asks.

"She's off-limits, asshole," I tell him sternly.

He puts his hands up like he's surrendering. "Got it."

I look over at the glass again, and my eyes land on Courtney's. She lights up with a smile that feels like it's just for me. I have to break eye contact as the line moves forward, and I roll into the next drill.

As the timer on warm-ups ticks down, the guys all start to head off the ice. I skate back over to the corner, I feel the need to talk to them both one final time before I have to get my head fully in game mode.

"Did you have fun?" I ask Jax.

"Yes! Is that all?" he asks.

I chuckle. "No, buddy, that was just us warming

up. We'll be back out to play the game in about twenty minutes or so. Now, you and Mom can go find your seats and maybe get a snack," I say to Jax. "You good with finding your seats?" I ask Courtney.

"Yep, I'm good."

"If it isn't too late, you can stick around after the game and I can catch up with you guys. It might be forty minutes or so before I get out, so I understand if that's too long."

"Probably will be too late. Jax is used to going to bed around nine, but maybe another time," she suggests.

"No problem," I tell her as the buzzer goes off, alerting me that I need to get off the ice so the ice crew can get it ready for the game. "That's my cue. I have to go. Have fun, and I'll see y'all later." I wave as I skate backward toward the bench. Once I reach the doorway, I turn around and head down the tunnel and into the locker room. As I enter the locker room, my mind immediately clicks to game mode.

I HOP OVER THE BOARDS, CHASING DOWN THE Florida winger as he pushes into the zone. I tie him up along the boards, digging at the puck until it pops free.

I tap it up the boards, hoping one of my teammates gathers it and gets it out of the zone.

I follow the play, getting into position to gain our offensive zone, watching as Graham clears the blue line, keeping us onside and in play. I skate down the boards and in toward the net, hoping that Graham will have an open slot where he can pass to me. Unfortunately, we're a second or two off, and the puck is just out of my reach as it slides into the corner. Caden, my center, drops down and collects the puck, bringing it back up to the point to set up the play. Graham and I drop into our positions as the wingers on this line, playing a game of keep away as we pass the puck between the three of us and work to find an open slot to try to score. The puck effortlessly slides from stick to stick as we work the ice. Caden fakes the pass to me and sends a slap shot toward the net and finds the smallest slot to put it into the back of the net. The goal horn blares as the five of us come together to celebrate, then head to the bench for the fist-bump line.

We take our one-goal lead into the third period. Florida is hot on our heels to tie up the game, but on the second shift of the third period, the fourth line buries the puck in the back of the net. Everyone on the bench stands and cheers loudly, celebrating the insurance that Jonesy provides with his goal.

Florida tries hard to beat Elijah, but we hold them off and shut them out with a final score of two to zero.

The atmosphere in the locker room buzzes with excitement the way it always is after a hard-fought win. Our goalie getting that shutout is icing on the cake in a big win. I quickly strip out of my gear and head for the showers. Even though I know Courtney won't be waiting outside for me, I still rush to get out of here. I want to call her and see how Jax liked the game and what he thought of it.

"Where's the fire?" Jonesy asks when I come out of the shower and head to get dressed.

"No fire, just ready to get home and relax," I tell him.

"Sure. We saw that hot chick you were talking to. It looked pretty comfortable for there to be nothing going on between the two of you."

"Just a friend," I say, not sure if I'm trying to convince them or myself about that.

"Famous last words."

I push out of the locker room, and even though I know Courtney and Jax won't be out here, I'm still disappointed I don't get to see them again. I slide my cell from my suit pocket and check for any missed calls or texts.

MOM

Great game tonight! Will you and
Sawyer be at dinner tomorrow night?

DAD

Looking good out there. Keep it up
and you guys have a good shot at
winning it all this season.

I chuckle at my dad's optimism, but he isn't wrong, either. We've been working our asses off as a team, and our current record proves that. We just need to keep that momentum going through the rest of the season.

ZACK

Thanks, Mom. I'm not sure about
Sawyer. I need to ask Emerson what
time she thinks they'll return from the
tournament. I haven't checked to see
what time his game is yet.

MOM

His team plays in the championship
at noon.

ZACK

My guess then is he won't be with
me. Anything I can bring?

MOM

Nope, just come hungry. Dad already
has the smoker going with the
brisket on.

ZACK

My stomach is already growling. I'll
be there by four thirty.

> MOM
> Perfect, see you then.

I reach my car and touch the handle, unlocking the doors. I open the back passenger door and toss my bag on the back seat, then remove my suit jacket and lay it over the top of the bag. I already have the top two buttons of my dress shirt undone, but I unbutton the cuffs and roll my sleeves up before I slide behind the wheel and ready myself to pull out of my spot. I wave at my teammates in the parking lot who are heading in their own directions as I pull out.

My car alerts me that I have a new text message and offers to read it to me. I tap the button on the screen on my dash, and the robotic voice comes over the speakers.

> COURTNEY
> Just wanted to say thank you again for the amazing time tonight. Jax was enthralled with everything that happened tonight. He even took his puck to bed with him.

Since I can't text her back, I hit the call button instead.

"Hello?" Courtney's sweet voice fills my car.

"Hey, I didn't want you to think I was ignoring you,

but I'm driving and couldn't text back, so I called instead."

"No problem."

"So you were saying that Jax had a great time. How about you?" I ask, hoping she enjoyed herself.

"It was a great night. I loved experiencing it through his eyes for the first time."

"I'm glad to hear that. Anytime the two of you want to go to another game, just let me know. I have vouchers for every game."

"Thank you," she says. "Where are you headed?"

"Home. I don't usually go out after games like some of the guys do."

"Ah."

"What does that mean?"

"Nothing. I just assumed that you'd be going out, being a bachelor and all that."

"Not really my thing anymore. As I've aged, I've come to enjoy being at home. I also try to have time with Sawyer whenever I can."

"You seem to have a good relationship with Emerson. Has it always been that way?" she asks.

"Yes, when we broke up, we decided to make Sawyer our priority. He shouldn't suffer just because we weren't meant to be together. We drew up a parenting plan, custody agreement, child support, everything that we could think of, and my attorney filed it with the courts. Since we'd come up with all of it together, it was a seamless process that the judge signed off on without any hesitation. It also went through quickly since we weren't married, so there was no marriage to dissolve."

"I'm scared how much of a fight it'll be with Chad," she says, and I can hear the trepidation in her words.

"Did you talk to Erin this week?" I ask, referring to my attorney.

"Yes, I had a call with her yesterday, and she said she'd contact Chad's attorney and discuss with him what Chad's demands are and see if we can agree on things outside of the courtroom."

"I told you she was great."

"I still don't know how I'm going to afford her services," Courtney whispers.

"Please don't worry about that. Let me help you through this."

"Why do you want to help so badly?"

"I can't explain it, Court, but it just feels like the right thing to do. I care about you and want to see you succeed in life. You've spent too many years under that asshole's thumb, and it's time you break out of your shell and shine. Find what you love in life and go after it."

I can hear her sniffle through my speakers, and my

heart breaks for her. I want to pull her into my arms and not let go.

"Have you already gone to bed, or are you still up?" I ask.

"I'm still up. Why?"

"Then open your door," I tell her.

"Open my door?" she says, the statement coming out like a question.

I turn off my car and pull my cell up to my ear so I can hear her. I step out of my car and lock the door.

"Are you really here?" she asks.

"Open your door and find out."

I walk the short distance to her apartment door, and just as I step up to it, I hear the lock slide as she flips it, and the door opens slowly. I end the call and slip the phone into my suit pants.

I push the door open wider, taking in Courtney in her sleep set. The low-cut tank shows off her breasts, and her hard nipples poke through the fabric. The sweats are tight and mold to every curve of her body. My desire for her takes over, and I shut the door behind me, then push her up against the wall. My lips crash against hers as her fingers tangle in my hair, pulling me closer as our tongues twist together.

Courtney lifts a leg, hooking it around my hip as she seeks friction between her legs. My body responds to her, and I press my pelvis against her center. As she moves, her pussy drags along my hard cock, and I want nothing more than to sink inside her body and make her scream my name.

I break our kiss, taking my lips to her neck as I kiss a trail down, then across the tops of her breasts. I pull the strap of her tank off her shoulder, and it slips down, exposing her breast to me fully. I lap at her hard nipple before sucking it between my lips. Courtney holds the back of my head to her as I devour her breast.

"Zack." Her breathy moans fill my ears. "I need you," she tells me.

I release her breast and stand back up to my full height. "Let me make you feel good tonight," I say as I slide a finger down her cheek. She grips my hand and pulls me down the hall and into her bedroom. Once we're in the room, she turns, and I can see the nervousness coursing through her body.

I grip her hips, aligning us to face one another. I tip her chin up so we can look into one another's eyes. I want to make sure she won't regret any of this tomorrow morning. "You are in control of everything tonight. If you want to stop at any point, speak up. Understand, sweetheart?" I ask, leaving no room for error.

She nods in agreement, but that isn't enough for me. "I need your words tonight, Court."

"I understand," she whispers.

I lower my head slowly, giving her time to stop me if she doesn't want me to kiss her again. She doesn't even flinch, so I continue, capturing her lips with my own. I continue to kiss her as I back her up and easily set her down on the mattress. I snag the hem of her top and pull it up, only breaking our kiss so I can pull it over her head. With her top off, I lay her back on the bed and map her body with my lips. I worship her breasts now that I have full access. They are the perfect size, filling my palm, but not so big I get lost in them.

I move on, sliding down farther, kissing along her torso, around her belly button, and down to the elastic band of her sleep pants. "May I?" I ask as I slip a fingertip under the edge.

"Yes," Courtney says as she lifts her hips. I don't hesitate to pull down her pants and panties at the same time. I toss them aside, then place her legs over my shoulders. I settle in, getting comfortable. I can see her arousal glistening on her slit, and my mouth waters with my desire to taste her and watch as she falls apart on my tongue.

I gently slide a fingertip down her seam, teasing her as I do. I chuckle at the way her body jolts at the touch, but relish in the way she moans in pleasure.

"Yes, more," Courtney whispers.

I flick out my tongue, tracing the same line I just

made with my fingertip. "Like that?" I ask before I part her and swirl my tongue around her clit. I slip two fingers inside her pussy, and her walls flutter around my digits as I make a come-here motion.

"Zack," she cries out in pure pleasure.

I release her clit but don't let up with my fingers. Her body practically vibrates with her need to come. "Shh, sweetheart, we don't want to wake up Jax," I warn.

She grabs the second pillow on the bed and places it over her face, I'm guessing to help block the sounds she's making. I return my mouth to her clit, alternating between sucking and flicking it with my tongue until she's riding my face and coming. Her body goes rigid, and I lap up every last drop of her release while she languishes in her post-orgasmic bliss. I slide up the bed, settling in on my side as I face her and wait for her to come back to me.

Her eyes finally find mine, and she's never been more beautiful. I run my fingers down the side of her face, cupping her cheek before I press a light kiss to her lips. "You're gorgeous when you come," I say against her lips. "I could watch you do that a million times over and never tire of it."

"Mhmm, that doesn't sound like a bad idea," she hums against my lips.

Courtney reaches out and unbuttons my dress

shirt, but I cover her hand and stop her. "Not tonight, sweetheart."

"What? Why not?" she asks, a little stunned that I'm stopping her from undressing me.

"This was all about you tonight. I want you to be completely mine when I sink inside you for the first time."

"But you need a release." She motions to my very tented slacks.

"Nothing I haven't dealt with before on my own." I smirk before kissing her again.

Courtney pushes me back and slides out of bed. I watch as she makes her way to the bathroom. She looks over her shoulder before clicking the door shut. I hear the toilet flush a minute later and the sink turn on. She emerges a few seconds later and scoops up her tank top and panties and pulls both back on before she joins me on the bed.

We lazily kiss, with no urgency to our movements, as we explore one another's bodies with our hands.

We naturally break apart, and I push a lock of hair out of Courtney's face. "I leave on Monday for a road trip and won't be back for a week, but once I am, I'd like to take you out on a date, if you're up to it."

"A date, huh?" She smiles at me.

"Yep." I pop the p. "I don't know what's changed between the two of us, but I know that I want to explore whatever this is. I understand if you want to take things slow. Just like tonight, you'll be in charge of how fast and far we move."

"I don't even know what to think about this," she says, and I know she's vulnerable at this moment. "What will Ryan think?"

"Let me deal with Ryan," I tell her. I know my best friend, and while he might not be ecstatic that I'd like to date his sister, he also knows the kind of man I am and that I'd never do anything to hurt her or Jax.

I can tell she's hesitant about that idea but eventually concedes. "Okay, but please don't ruin your relationship with my brother because of me. Especially since we have no idea what this is between us."

"Don't you worry your pretty little self about my relationship with Ryan. We're good, and he'll deal with it just fine," I say before kissing the tip of her nose.

Courtney yawns, which makes me look at the clock. It's well after midnight, and I know Jax will probably be up early tomorrow. "I should probably head home so you can get to sleep."

"Yeah, Jax is an early riser, especially on the weekends. I swear his internal clock only works on the days I'd like for him to sleep in."

"Sawyer is the same way. Maybe when I get back, we can plan something with the boys. Let them meet, which will allow us to spend more time together."

"I'd like that, but I have one request," Courtney says.

"What is your request?"

"When we're around the kids, we keep things PG. I don't want to confuse him, and I think him seeing me with a man right now might do that. I know he's comfortable around you and already likes you, but I think we need to take things slow."

"I can agree to those terms. Like I said, you're in control, sweetheart."

"Are you sure you're real?" Courtney pinches my side.

"Ouch," I yelp, then immediately cover my mouth with a hand.

"Sorry." She laughs. "I just had to check for myself."

"Like the orgasm I just gave you wasn't enough of the real thing?" I quirk an eyebrow at her as I roll her on her back and kiss her hard. I slip my tongue past her lips and tangle it with hers before abruptly pulling away, leaving us both panting and wanting more.

I slide off the bed but don't take my eyes off Courtney. I get my fill of her beautiful body, which is still mostly on display.

She sits up and slides off the bed, bending down to grab her sleep pants that she didn't put back on earlier. Once she pulls them on, I snag her hand, linking our fingers together. "Walk me out?" I ask.

We make our way out of her room and down the short hall to the entryway.

"When do you leave on Monday?" she asks.

"I think I have to be at the airport around nine, maybe nine thirty."

"And you'll be gone an entire week?"

I tuck her hair behind each ear, then drop my hands to her hips. "Yes, Monday to Monday this time. We have four games while we're gone. Tuesday and Wednesday, then Friday and Sunday, before returning on Monday. We're going to Seattle first, then Vancouver, then Edmonton and Calgary."

"Sounds like a cold trip."

"Definitely." I chuckle. "Visiting any of the northern teams in the winter can sure be a shock to the system sometimes."

"Be safe, and text me if you have time."

"Every night. You can text me, too, anytime. If I'm busy, I'll get back to you when I'm off the ice. That's really the only time I'm away from my phone."

"You sure? That won't cramp your style?" she asks.

"I wouldn't have told you to if I didn't want to hear from you. Just like I didn't go out with the guys tonight, I don't usually go out for more than dinner and maybe a drink in the hotel bar if I'm feeling up to it one night on the road trip. I usually hang out with the guys during the day and then keep my nights open to talk to

Sawyer when he's free, which isn't all that long between his school day, dinner, hockey practice, and a reasonable bedtime."

"I can't even imagine what it would be like with Jax in a competitive sport. Our evenings are already busy enough, and we basically just come home and have dinner."

"You've got time. Do you think he's interested in any particular sport?"

"After tonight, hockey." She laughs.

"Touché."

"Will you text me when you get home so I know you made it safe?"

"I can do that," I agree before I pull her in for one last kiss.

6

COURTNEY

I stare at my door after Zack leaves and I've locked up. I'm still shell-shocked over the way the evening panned out. I never would have guessed he'd end up at my place, nor that we would have kissed or done everything else we did.

My body still hums from his touch and the pleasure he showed me. The exhaustion sets in, so I turn to head for bed. I stop in the kitchen and fill up my water bottle to take it with me to my bedroom. I drink greedily from the bottle as I stand next to my rumpled bed. Once I set the water bottle on my nightstand, I find the pillows and blankets before sliding between the sheets. I can smell Zack's cologne on my sheets, so I pull in a deep breath, letting his smell fill my lungs.

I pull out my Kindle, needing something to keep me awake until Zack gets home and texts me that he made it safely. I get pulled into the book I'm reading until my vibrating phone startles me.

> ZACK
>
> I made it home. Sleep well, sweetheart.

> COURTNEY
>
> I'm already tucked into bed and was just reading until you texted. Good night, Zack. Thanks for coming over.

> ZACK
>
> Thanks for opening your door and not kicking me right back out after I kissed you in the entryway.

> COURTNEY
>
> Are you going to be okay with your situation?

> ZACK
>
> I'll be fine, sweetheart. I'll just think of you coming on my tongue, and I'll come like a geyser. (smile emoji) (devil face emoji) I thought my problem would have gone away on my drive home, but apparently not, as this evidence shows: {Picture of tented slacks}

> COURTNEY
>
> I still think you should have let me take care of that for you.

> ZACK
>
> Next time.

>   COURTNEY
>
>   I'm holding you to that. {winky kissy
>   face}

> ZACK
>
> Whatever you say, sweetheart.

>   COURTNEY
>
>   Not to cut this short, but I'm having a
>   hard time keeping my eyes open. I
>   need to go to sleep.

> ZACK
>
> Sweet dreams. Text me once you're
> up and about.

>   COURTNEY
>
>   Will do. Good night, Zack.

I plug my phone in and set it on the nightstand. I hear it vibrate against the wood, but my eyes are already closed, so I leave it for the morning.

"WHAT HAS YOU SO SMILEY TODAY?" RYAN ASKS. We sit on his patio as Jax runs around playing.

"Nothing specific, just starting to feel like myself again."

"I'm proud of you for getting out of a bad situation."

"Thanks," I tell my brother. "How was your date?"

"It was good. We're going out again later this week."

"And how did you meet this girl?"

"One of my clients set me up. It's his cousin. She just moved to town a few months ago and is trying to meet people."

"And her name?" I ask. Getting information out of my brother can be like pulling teeth sometimes.

"Allison. She's twenty-eight and is a counselor focusing on adolescents and young adults."

"She sounds great and sounds like she's got a good career path."

"She's wicked smart, down to earth, and beautiful in that natural way. She doesn't try too hard like a lot of women do. She reminds me of you, actually."

I scrunch my nose and look at my brother. "Eww, I hope you aren't attracted to women who remind you of me."

Ryan tosses a napkin at me, but it drops on the ground before it even reaches me. "Not physically, brat. Just her determination and how she's handled situations that have come up in her life."

"Does she have kids?" I ask.

"No."

"Well, I'm happy for you if it works out, and I look forward to meeting her when the time is right."

"What about you? Do you think you'll date again?" I can feel my ears and cheeks heat, and I'm sure they are burning red.

"Eventually, yes, I could see myself dating and settling down with someone who treats me right. He'll have to understand that Jax is my top priority and will always come first. So if I can find someone who fits that bill, then yes, I'd like to be in a relationship again."

"No one out there will ever be good enough for you," Ryan grumbles.

"If that's the case, then there's no guy in the world who is good enough for any woman, and that goes for you and Allison," I state, giving him my stern mom look.

He holds up his hands in surrender. "I see your point." He rubs his chin and cheek with his hand as he ponders his words. "I think it's just the older brother protective instinct to think that about you, especially knowing the relationship you just left behind. I can't tell you how many times I wanted to drive across this state and give Chad someone his own size to pick on. The things he put the two of you through aren't normal or something you do to your loved ones."

"I know, and it's why I finally left. But I'm safe. Jax is safe. We're here now and not leaving."

"Any progress with the attorney and the custody issues?" Ryan asks.

"I talked to Zack's attorney last week, and she's reaching out to Chad's attorney to see if we can get him to agree to mediation and keep this out of the courts.

I'm hopeful he's on board with that as it should be a lot cheaper for both of us with legal fees."

"Do you know how much you have to come up with right away?" he asks.

"She said nothing is required as Zack has her on retainer. I tried to argue, but she wouldn't let up and give me a dollar amount."

"He's one of the few good guys I know," Ryan says, and I can feel myself relax at his words. If he knows the kind of man Zack is deep down, then maybe he won't freak out when the time comes to tell him we've been seeing one another. I'm trying not to let my hopes get ahead of me too far, knowing all too well that this could be just a fling that only lasts a short time.

"He sure is," I agree and hope I'm not on fire for not telling my brother all the details from the past few days.

I'M READING *FROGGY GOES TO SCHOOL* FOR THE third night in a row as it is Jax's current favorite book—well, at least for this week—when my phone vibrates in my pocket.

"Who's calling you, Mommy?" Jax asks.

"Not sure, but I can call them back after we're done."

"What if it's Uncle Ryan?"

I pull my phone out of my pocket and see Zack's face on my screen.

"Zack?!" Jax asks, excitement filling his voice. "Answer it, Mommy. I want to say hi."

I slide the bar across the screen to answer the call. "Hello, you're on speakerphone, and Jax is in my lap," I warn quickly so he doesn't say something inappropriate for little ears.

"Hey, buddy," he says to Jax.

"Zack, are you playing hockey today?" he asks.

"Not today, we got today off, but I still have a game tomorrow night and one on Sunday before I'll be back home. Did you watch my game on TV last night?"

"A little, but Mom made me go to bed because it was my bedtime."

"Yeah, sometimes my games are late, especially when I'm gone and having to play in different time zones. Speaking of late, are you getting off to bed?"

"We were almost done with his bedtime book when you called," I tell Zack. "Jax insisted I answer your call so he could say hi to you."

"Ah, well let me let you go then. Call me later?" he asks.

"Yep, give me a half hour or so."

"I'll be waiting," he confirms before the line goes dead. I turn back to the book and pick up right where we left off.

Once I've finished the book, I move over so Jax can get himself situated fully under his blankets. "I love you to the moon and back," I say like I've done since the day he was born. Whenever I put him down for a nap or bed, I tell him those eight words.

"Moon and back," he replies with half-closed eyes. I press a kiss to his cheek and get up and walk to the door. Before I pull it closed behind me, I stare at my son in his bed. He looks so peaceful. About a week after we moved back, he stopped waking up at night, which had been an almost nightly occurrence. He stopped having accidents at night and has started to thrive overall. I can only attribute that to no longer being in an environment where we are always afraid of what kind of mood Chad would be in. Never knew if he'd be sober, or drunk and high.

I fill up my water bottle before heading into my bathroom and drawing a bath. Once I have the tub filled, I sink into the hot water. I prop my phone up on the tray that fits across the tub and tap Zack's contact.

"Hey, gorgeous," he says as he answers the call. "Can I FaceTime you? I want to see your beautiful face tonight."

"Umm..." I hesitate.

"What's wrong?" He's instantly on high alert.

"Nothing bad. I'm just soaking in the tub. It's why I needed a little bit to call you back."

"Fuck me," he says under his breath.

"What was that?" I ask.

"Nothing, sweetheart. I was already at half-mast just hearing your voice. Seeing you naked will make me as hard as steel," he says.

"Then we don't have to switch to the video," I say, knowing damn well he won't let that slide.

My screen flashes with the notification that he's requested to change the call over. I chuckle as I accept the video call and wait for the few seconds it takes for our cameras to start working correctly. The way my phone is propped up in the holder, you can only see from about my collarbone up.

"Any chance you can lower that camera?" Zack asks. I can practically feel his smolder through the damn phone.

I adjust it ever so slightly, giving him another inch or so of skin, but not what he really wants—my breasts.

"Damn, you take my breath away." I tap my phone to make the little box that shows what he's seeing larger, so I can see myself through his eyes. I just see a tired mom relaxing in a bath.

"How was your free day?" I ask, not really sure what else to say to his last statement.

"It was good. Went down for some treatment. I have a hip flexor that is causing some problems. Nothing that a few extra stretches and some time with one of the trainers massaging it out won't cure."

"With today being an off day, does that mean no practice, as well?"

"Just kind of depends on the day, where we're at in our schedule, how many guys we've got out on injury. The list goes on and on. There was a short optional skate, but I didn't go. Treatment was my priority today."

"Will you be okay for tomorrow's game?" I ask.

"Oh yeah, I'll be fine. The trainers will stretch me out really well tomorrow afternoon. I probably won't even notice the nagging injury during the game."

"Is it something you've dealt with for a long time?"

"It pops up every season or so. Sometimes it goes away after a few days, and other times, it sticks around for weeks or months. Just depends on how many hits I take."

"I still can't fully wrap my mind around how physically demanding your job is," I admit.

"Don't you worry, it has also built up my stamina." He winks.

"Ugh, you're incorrigible." I slosh the water around a little as I shift in the tub.

"I'm feeling a little overdressed this evening," he

says, and moves on his bed. He reaches behind his head and grips his T-shirt. He pulls it up and over his head, all in one movement. His chiseled torso fills my screen, and I might start to drool when I get a good look at the ridges of his abs. "Like what you see?" he asks. I slowly drag my eyes to meet his, finding a cocky smirk on his lips. One that I'd really like to kiss off.

"I don't just like what I see. I'm a little fonder of it now that I'm getting a good look."

"Want me to keep going?" he offers, sliding his hand down his abdomen.

"No!" I adamantly state. "I'm not having sexy times over FaceTime."

He pouts slightly but quickly brushes it off. "I understand."

"But do you?" I ask with a laugh.

"I do. It doesn't mean I wouldn't take advantage of the situation should it present itself to me," he quips.

"Spoken like a true red-blooded man," I tease. "Sex, sports, and food are the top three things on your mind at any moment, am I right?"

"Pretty much. There are times when other things are on my mind, but those three are normally at the top of the list."

"Oh, I meant to tell you something. When I was over at Ryan's place, we talked about his date, and then he asked me if I thought I'd ever want to date again. I treaded very carefully, never mentioning anything about you and me. But he made a strange, yet good, comment. He said you're one of the few good guys he knows. I think that's a good omen for the two of us, especially if and when it's time for you to have a little talk with him if we continue whatever this is," I say as I motion to both of us.

"Good to know. Did he say how his date went?" Zack asks.

"Said it went well. They're going out again, so that's a good sign. He seemed to really like her."

"That's good. He needs a good woman in his life. One who balances him out and can put him in his place a time or two."

"Something like that. So what's your schedule like for tomorrow?" I ask.

"Morning skate will probably only be on the ice for forty-five minutes, at most. Followed by some treatment, then back to the hotel for lunch and a pre-game nap, then back to the rink by four. Since we're on the road, we all arrive at the same time via motor coach. Then, off-ice warm-ups, stretching, all the normal pre-game stuff until it's time to hit the ice."

"I'm going to surprise Jax with some pizza on the way home so we can have it while we watch the game on TV. We're going to stop at Target, as well, so he can pick out a special treat for dessert, and we'll make a fun night out of it."

"I love that."

"My plan is during the second intermission, we'll take care of bath time and get into pj's, then stay up a little late to watch the final period."

"I'm sure he'll be ecstatic."

"Yep, but that is also why I'm not telling him my plan until after I pick him up from after-school care."

"Smart woman." I sit up and reach for the drain plug, flipping it open so the tub drains.

"Are you getting out?" he asks.

"Yeah, I'm well pruned up." I flip my phone over so the camera is face down on my bath tray. I don't need to flash him while I'm trying to get out of the tub and dry off.

"Hey," he objects.

"You'll get over it. This isn't flattering at all."

"Nothing I haven't seen already."

I can't help but laugh at his words. "Seeing me the way you did the other night is different."

"How so?" he asks as I pick the phone back up. I have my robe on and tied tight.

"I can't explain it, but it just is, okay?"

"Okay," he says with a puffed-out lower lip, like he's a toddler pouting.

"I'm immune to pouts," I tease.

"Well, that's no fun. How am I supposed to get you to bend to my requests?"

I smile at him. "I guess you'll just have to figure it out."

I love our easy banter and flirting. Zack makes me feel so relaxed and like I'm important, and that feeling just does something to my insides.

"Where'd you just go?" he asks.

"Nowhere. Just enjoying this feeling," I tell him honestly.

"Fuck, I wish I was there and could kiss you right now."

"Maybe you can come over on Monday night," I suggest.

"Yes, what time will you be home? I'll bring dinner with me so you don't have to cook."

"Probably six or shortly after."

"I'll be there waiting."

"I look forward to it," I tell him.

We continue to talk for another half hour or so as I get ready for bed. My alarm goes off early tomorrow, so I need to get to sleep.

"Sweet dreams, sweetheart."

"Thanks. Sweet dreams yourself. Talk soon." We disconnect the call, and I fall back on my pillow. The giddy feelings haven't gone away. If anything, they've gotten stronger.

7

ZACK

The past month has flown by. Somehow, we've already reached the week of the trade deadline. A week that always has so many guys on the edge of their seats. I remember those days, never knowing if you were going to get the call that you had to pack your shit and get on the next flight to a new city.

Thankfully, with my last contract extension, I was able to negotiate in a no-trade clause. I wanted to be close to Sawyer, and that was my guarantee that I would be with him as much as possible.

Coach walks into the locker room. "Listen up," he calls out, and everyone stops talking and turns their attention to him. "I know this week is stressful. We've got twenty-four hours left until the deadline. I know the suits have some cards still at play, and some deals might still come through. No matter who walks through that door"—he pauses and points behind him at the door—"we're a team. We have one another's backs at all times. I know this isn't new for any of you. You've all been through trades at some point in your careers. Whatever happens, happens, and we keep moving forward toward the ultimate goal of raising that Cup at the end of the season."

"Hell yeah, Coach," Easton calls out, and the room erupts in laughter. Coach chuckles and shakes his head at Easton.

"I'll see you all out on the ice in ten," Coach says before turning and leaving the room.

We all finish getting ready. I can see the look in the guys' eyes who are rumored to be on the trade block. I feel for them. That uncertainty can be so nerve-racking, not to mention how much harder it is if you have a family you have to worry about moving.

We hit the ice, and Coach runs us hard. I think he does so to help guys get the deadline off their minds. The shrill of the whistle blows again. "Again," Coach yells from the center of the ice. "Pick up your feet, Kaden. You're getting sloppy on me."

"Fuck off," he grumbles from next to me.

"Don't let Coach hear you say that," I warn him.

"I'm going to fucking puke," he tells me. "I haven't

had to do bag skates like this since early in my junior years."

"It's good for you," I tell him as I suck in a lungful of air. He isn't wrong. I also haven't had to do a bag skate like this one in a long-ass time. I'll be so ready for the ice bath when I hit the locker room.

The shrill of the whistle blows again, but this time, Coach doesn't make us skate back to the other end. "Good job, men," he says, motioning for us to join him at center ice. We all slowly push off and skate to surround him. Everyone takes a knee, some out of respect to Coach, but mostly because our legs feel like limp noodles. "I'm proud of all of you. You didn't quit when it got hard, even if you wanted to. You dug deep and found the will to keep pushing. That's the kind of dedication and heart we need to push to the end of the season. Now go, get out of here. Relax and spend time with your families. You have tomorrow off. Training staff will be here if you need them. Otherwise, I don't want to see your faces until the day after tomorrow. We'll regroup and see where we stand at that time."

We make our way off the ice and into the locker room. The room is quiet compared to normal. I strip out of my gear and sit on the seat of my locker. I greedily suck down the recovery drink our training staff left in my space. They take care of us, making sure we have what we need before and after being on the ice.

Once I have drunk the first smoothie, I switch to the electrolyte drink and drain that in a few gulps. I grab my towel and head for the ice bath. My muscles are already screaming at me from today's practice, so a good soak will do them some good. I sink into the ice-cold water, my body instantly shivering as the cold envelops me. I can feel my balls shriveling up into my body as they seek warmth. My mind instantly travels to Courtney and thoughts of her in my bed. We still haven't made it there, but it will happen. I have faith that we will get to where we both want our relationship to go. Building our friendship has been an important step, and I know she needs things to go slow. She hasn't been out of her relationship with Chad for long, so I'm willing to give her all the time she needs to feel ready. Especially when she lets me kiss her when no one is looking.

"Hey, sweetheart," I say when the call connects.

"Hi, how was your day?" Courtney asks.

"Practice was rough, but we made it through."

"Ah, what are you up to now?"

"I'm waiting for Sawyer's practice to end, then we're headed home for some dinner. Any chance I can convince you to come over with Jax to join us? Coach gave us tomorrow off, so I'm all yours until the day after tomorrow."

"Sure, when will you be home? And can I bring anything?" she offers.

"Just the two of you, and his practice ends in about five minutes. It should take him ten or fifteen minutes in the locker room. We can be home in thirty, maybe forty minutes."

"Perfect. I'm on my way to pick up Jax now. We'll meet you at your place."

"See you then," I say before we disconnect the call. Knowing I'll get to see her tonight has my day turning right around. Just as I slip my phone into my pocket, it vibrates with an incoming text, so I pull it back out to see who it's from.

> RYAN
>
> Hey man, what's up?

> ZACK
>
> Not a whole lot, just hockey, hockey, and more hockey.

ZACK

RYAN

I bet. I just saw the newest trade
rumor. Wouldn't that be sweet if it's
true?

ZACK

I haven't paid any attention to
anything going on. I don't like to
focus on the what-ifs.

RYAN

Camden freaking Rowe is rumored to
be coming here from San Francisco.

ZACK

No shit? He's fucking good. Who's
going?

I worry slightly as I run through my teammates and wonder who we have to give up to get Camden.

RYAN

This report is just talking about some
draft picks and maybe a few guys
down in the AHL.

ZACK

That would be fucking amazing.

RYAN

I'll keep a watch on it and let you
know if they say anything more about
it. What else is shaking?

ZACK

Not a whole lot, just at Sawyer's practice. It just ended, so we're headed home for some dinner. He's got school tomorrow, so nothing crazy going on tonight. I have practice on Saturday, but nothing in the evening. We should get together unless you've got a hot date? I'll have Sawyer again since he's actually home for once when I am, so it'd need to be kid-friendly.

RYAN

I'd be down for sure. I can introduce you to Allison. Hell, maybe I should have Courtney and Jax come at the same time. Get introductions over with all at once.

ZACK

Whatever you want to do, man. Courtney and I met up a few weeks ago so the boys could meet. They got along great, so I'm down for anything. What about Topgolf? Sawyer has been begging me to take him there again.

RYAN

Sure. What time?

ZACK

I'll call and see what time we can get a bay. Maybe shoot for around five or six? We can order dinner and drinks while hanging out.

> RYAN
>
> Sounds like a plan.

>> ZACK
>>
>> Sawyer's on his way out of the locker room, so I'll catch you later once I have a time nailed down.

I slip my phone back into my pocket as Sawyer runs up to me. "Dad, did you see my nasty goal?"

"Sure did. You looked good out there." I rub the top of his sweaty head. "Missed you this week, kiddo."

"Dad," he grumbles as he shakes off my hand.

"Zack." I hear someone calling my name. I look up and see Sawyer's head coach jogging down the hall in our direction.

"Carter," I greet him, offering my hand for him to shake. "Nice to see you."

"Glad I caught you. I wanted to ask if you'd be available to help out with a clinic we're planning during spring break. I looked at your game schedule, and depending on your practice schedule, I'm hoping Wednesday of that week would work for you to come out for a few hours."

"I'm happy to help. Can you shoot me a text with the details? I'll check and get back to you. Do you want a few of us, if possible?"

"The more the merrier, but no pressure if it doesn't work."

"I don't see why I can't at least come. Even if it's after practice, if I can't get out of it."

"Thanks. I'll text you the information when I get home."

"Sounds good. Have a good night, Carter."

Sawyer slings his bag over his shoulder, and I take his sticks from him. "You ready for some dinner?" I ask as we make it out to my truck.

"Yes, I'm starving," he says, exaggerating the sentence.

"You make it sound like you haven't eaten in a week, and I know damn sure your mom packed you a snack to eat before practice."

"Gross veggies and dip," he grumbles.

"Junk food won't keep you fueled on the ice."

He mumbles some more, but I don't catch what he says.

We both get settled into the truck, and I crank the engine. He's focused on drinking the electrolyte drink I grabbed for him and had waiting in the cup holder.

"I invited Courtney and Jax over for dinner tonight," I tell him as we drive home.

"Is she your girlfriend?" he asks.

I don't want to lie to him, but we haven't put any labels on what we are yet.

"No, not that she might not be, at some point. Right

now, we're just friends. Would you be okay with that if she was?" I ask.

He shrugs. "She's nice, and Jax isn't annoying."

I chuckle at his no-shit attitude. "I agree. Does it bother you that your mom and I are moving on?"

"No, Joe is great for Mom. She's happy, and that makes me happy," he says, referring to his stepdad. Emerson got married a few years ago after a few years of dating Joe.

"I agree, kiddo. Joe's been good for both of you."

"So if Courtney makes you happy, then that's okay with me," he says, and I wonder where this grown-up kid came from. It feels like he's ten going on twenty some days.

"I'll keep that in mind."

"Isn't she Uncle Ryan's sister?" he asks.

"Yep," I confirm, not like I can hide that fact from him. I can't ask him to lie about what he knows, so it sounds like I need to have a little chat with Ryan sooner than later about the possibility of Courtney and me being in a relationship.

We make it home a few minutes later, and Courtney's car is already in the driveway, waiting for us to get home. I pull into the garage and hop out.

"Zack, I got my own stick!" Jax yells as he runs my way after getting out of the car.

"You did? Let me see," I say. He holds up the mini stick that I'd ordered and had sent to their place. It came with a little net, some foam balls, and a couple of other sticks.

"That's a pretty sweet stick. Maybe you and Sawyer can play some knee hockey after we have dinner."

"Can I take a shower first?" Sawyer asks as he unloads his bag.

"Of course. Why don't you go run in and take one while I get dinner going."

I open the door from the garage to the house and motion for everyone to go in before me. The boys run inside, Jax on Sawyer's heels. I snag Courtney's hand as she passes by and hold her back. The door closes most of the way and I take advantage of the moment and press a kiss to her lips. "Hi," I whisper against her lips when we break apart.

"Hi." She smiles up at me.

"Sorry, I just couldn't resist any longer and didn't know if I'd get the opportunity again."

"I'm glad you did. I've missed you," she admits. I knew she did, she's told me daily when we've talked. It's been almost a week since we saw each other.

"I was texting with Ryan earlier and suggested we all get together on Saturday, maybe around five or so. I need to see if I can get us a reservation at *Topgolf*.

What do you say? Are you and Jax in? Ryan is going to bring Allison for us to meet."

"Is he now?" She purses her lips as we walk into my house. I head straight for the kitchen, and Courtney follows me. I pull out the package of chicken that has been marinating all day, along with my grilling tools. "Can I help with anything?"

"I have some macaroni salad in the fridge if you want to pull that out and give it a good mix. Then, there's also a bagged salad you can toss together. I'm going to go fire up the grill."

She heads to the fridge as I head outside. I give the grill a few minutes to heat before I get the chicken down on it to start cooking. I set the timer on my watch and head back inside to see how things are going in there. Jax is in the kitchen helping Courtney as she adds things to the salad bowl.

"Can I get either of you something to drink?" I offer.

"Already a step ahead of you." Courtney flashes me a smile over her shoulder. "I hope you don't mind that I helped ourselves to stuff in your fridge."

"Of course not. Whatever you want is free for the taking."

Sawyer joins us a moment later, his hair still dripping from his shower. "When will dinner be ready?" he asks.

"Another ten minutes or so for the chicken," I tell him, since I still need to flip it. Just then, the timer on my watch goes off, and I head outside to flip the food. Sawyer follows me outside and sits down on one of the chairs.

"Can we eat outside?" he asks.

"I suppose. Just turn on the outside lights as the sun has almost set, and it will be dark."

He heads inside and does as I asked. He returns with Courtney on his heels, her hands filled with the pasta and salad.

"I hear we're eating out here," she says. I grab one of the bowls out of her hands and set it on the table.

"It's a nice night, might as well take advantage of it."

"Of course," she agrees.

"Remind me later to expand on that," I quietly whisper so only Courtney hears, since both boys are now outside with us.

She gives me a curious look, but I don't elaborate.

The timer goes off once again. This time, the chicken is done, so I plate it up and take it to the table. In the meantime, Courtney brought out plates and silverware for all of us. It feels so natural for the four of us to sit down together for dinner.

We all make small talk while we eat. The boys each tell us about their days at school. Sawyer tells us about his tournament last weekend and the goals he scored. His team won another championship, adding to their tally for the season. If they keep it up, they'll end the season as the best team in their league.

Once we're all done eating, the boys go pull out the knee hockey stuff, and Sawyer helps teach Jax how to play as Courtney and I watch from where we're relaxing. "He's so good with him," Courtney says as she watches with pure happiness showing on her face.

"I agree. Oh, more about what I mentioned earlier. Sawyer asked me some interesting questions on the ride home after I told him the two of you were coming over. He also put two and two together and knows that you and Ryan are siblings. I think I'm going to have a conversation with Ryan before we get together on Saturday. I don't want Sawyer to say something and it get taken out of context or catch Ryan off guard."

Courtney blows out a breath before turning her eyes to mine. "And what are you planning on telling him?" she asks.

"The truth. That I'm incredibly infatuated with his sister, and I believe the feelings are mutual, but that we're taking things slow and seeing where they go. I'll be straight with him that I'm not looking for his permission to date you, but I hope he gives his blessing, especially knowing that we make one another happy when we're able to spend time together."

"Do you want me with you?" she asks.

"I've thought about it, and I think just him and I is the best. That way, if he flips out, he only does so on me."

"He's not going to freak out."

"I don't think he will, either, but just in case." I wink at her to try to lighten the mood.

"What happens after the conversation?" she asks.

"Whatever we want to happen."

"When's the next weekend night that you are home but don't have Sawyer?"

"I think next weekend, why?"

"Maybe I'll ask Ryan if he can keep Jax for me overnight, and I can come spend the night," she suggests.

"Yes, make it happen," I say, the words flying out of my mouth. "Ask for the entire weekend."

Courtney laughs. "We'll see. I don't want to push my luck, but maybe between him and my parents. I think they'll be back by then."

"If all you can do is one night, we'll make the most of it," I promise her. My dick hardens at the thought of having her all to myself for an entire night. My mind flashes back to that night I showed up at her place and got my first and only taste.

"What's that smirk for?" she asks.

"Just remembering my first taste of you and dreaming about it happening again." Courtney's cheeks instantly blush from my words, and I know I've hit my mark. "Don't worry, sweetheart. There'll be more of that, plus a whole lot more when I have you all to myself for an entire night. I'll have you screaming my name without a pillow over your face to hide your pleasure."

Courtney fans her face with her hand. "Damn, you sure do know how to tease a girl."

"No tease, honey. I'm all about promises to come. See what you do to me?" I say, pointing at the bulge in my pants.

"You going to be okay until next weekend?" She grimaces.

"I'll be just fine, unless you want to sneak away for a few minutes?" I quirk an eyebrow in question. Courtney's eyes flash over to where the boys are playing together, then pulls her bottom lip between her teeth, lightly chewing on it as she thinks.

"As much as I'd love that, I don't think now is the right time."

"It kills me to agree with you, but you're right. Will make next weekend all that much sweeter when the time comes."

"And you're sure you won't have Sawyer?" she asks.

"Positive. I have a home game on Friday night and he's got an out-of-town tournament that weekend, so he'll be with Emerson until sometime on Sunday."

"Did you want me to see if Ryan can take Jax on Saturday night then?"

"If you can only get one night, then yes, otherwise, you can come to my game, then we can head back here together afterward."

"I'll see what I can arrange," she promises.

8

COURTNEY

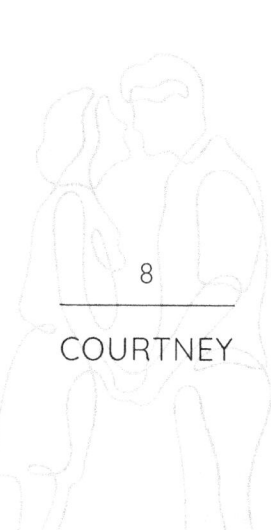

Jax and I hang out at Zack's until just after eight. I still need to get him home, into the shower, and off to bed. "Time to go, buddy. We have an early morning tomorrow, and it's almost bedtime."

"Okay," he grumbles, but helps Sawyer start to pick up the hockey stuff.

"I'll walk the two of you out," Zack says once we both have our shoes on and are ready to leave.

"Thanks," I tell him as he holds the door open for us. We walk through the garage and out to my car in the driveway. "Thanks for having us over. It was a great time, and dinner was amazing."

"Of course, thanks for coming. Did you have fun tonight, Jax?" Zack asks him.

"Yes," he says just before a yawn slips from his lips.

"You look tired, buddy. I'll let the two of you get going so you can get home and into bed."

"Okay," Jax agrees as he rests his head on me. I pick him up and place him in his booster seat in the back seat. I help him get buckled since he's so tired. I close the passenger door and step forward to the driver's door.

Zack beats me to opening my door. "Thanks for everything," I tell him.

"My pleasure. Let me know you've made it home safe?" he asks.

"Of course," I tell him before slipping behind the wheel. I'd love to have kissed him good night, but I'm not ready to cross that bridge around Jax quite yet.

COURTNEY

Favorite brother of mine…

RYAN

Oh god, what did you do?

COURTNEY

I didn't do anything (sticking tongue out emoji) I have a question for you. How much do you love me, and, well, your nephew?

RYAN

That was two questions. I'd do just about anything for that kid. You? Eh, depends on what it is. (Big smile emoji)

COURTNEY

I see how it is. I make you an uncle, and I'm just chopped liver now.

RYAN

Pretty much. So what's up? What do you need?

COURTNEY

What would it take to convince you to take Jax for next weekend?

RYAN

The entire weekend? Where are you going?

COURTNEY

If you're up for the entire weekend, then yes. If not, then at least most of Saturday until Sunday, maybe noonish? I'm trying to plan a date. I met someone, and we've been talking for a while. We'd like to spend the weekend together without kids. He won't have his son next weekend, so we thought it would be the perfect opportunity.

I know I'm being vague, but I don't want to spill that I'm talking about Zack just yet. I know he wanted to talk to him this weekend and be the one to break it to Ryan that we'd like to date one another.

> **RYAN**
>
> Do I get to meet this asshole who thinks he's good enough for you before you spend a weekend with him?
>
> **COURTNEY**
>
> I'll get back to you on that.
>
> **RYAN**
>
> To answer you, yes, I can take Jax for the weekend. I'm proud of you for getting yourself back out there. Just don't be shocked if I give him the older brother shakedown at some point.
>
> **COURTNEY**
>
> I wouldn't expect anything less from you. I'll get back to you on specifics. I can probably have them nailed down by tomorrow night when we meet up at Topgolf with Zack. I'm super excited to meet Allison!
>
> **RYAN**
>
> Sounds like a plan.

I close out my text message with my brother and open up the one I have with Zack.

COURTNEY

Just asked Ryan about next weekend. He's willing to keep Jax for me all weekend. His only request was getting to meet the guy I've been talking to and going out with. I told him I'd see what I can do and will let him know for sure tomorrow night.

ZACK

Fuck yes. Be ready for me next weekend. (Smirking devil face) I'll head over to his place after practice tomorrow and chat with him.

COURTNEY

I can't wait. (winky face) Please don't do anything rash.

ZACK

I'll be just fine. I can withstand the big brother stick.

COURTNEY

How'd it go today with the deadline?

ZACK

We got a shocking trade that came through this morning. We picked up a pretty big player from San Francisco. His name is Camden Rowe. Was definitely a shock. I know he was a fan favorite out there.

COURTNEY

I take it that was a good addition.

ZACK

Yes, very good. He's a top player in the league. I'm excited to get to know him once he gets here. Probably will arrive sometime late tonight or maybe tomorrow. They'll give him a little bit of extra time since we don't have another game for a few days.

COURTNEY

I find it fascinating learning how your world works. I don't think most people realize just how much goes on behind the scenes for a professional athlete.

ZACK

You are correct. Most people just see the game part, but there is so much more to it.

COURTNEY

I forgot to tell you, but I got a message from Erin Monroe. She needs me to come in next week so we can go over some stuff. She said she has until late next week to submit our answers, so I'm meeting her on Monday.

ZACK

Do you want me to come with you?

COURTNEY

That isn't necessary. It will be just her and me from what I know.

ZACK

Well, if that changes, let me know, and I'll see what I can do to help you out.

COURTNEY

I'm also going to submit my day off request for Saturday at The Burger Shack. I don't want anything in our way for next weekend.

ZACK

Perfect

COURTNEY

I have to go. My lunch break is over.

ZACK

Call me once you're off work.

COURTNEY

Sounds good. Talk soon.

I slip my phone back into my pocket and clean up my lunch mess. I toss stuff in the trash, then return my container to my lunch box so I can take it home and get it washed up.

9

ZACK

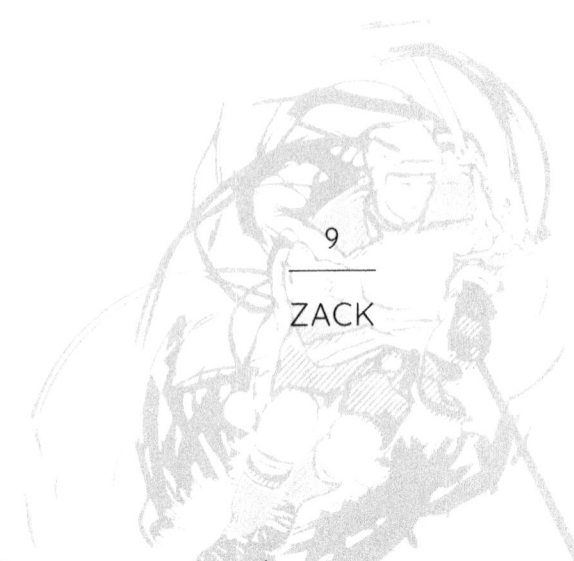

I pull into Ryan's driveway, parking along the outer edge. I kill the engine and head up to the house. I left Sawyer with my parents for a few hours. They wanted some grandparent time, and I needed to come take care of this.

I walk into his house, much like he usually just walks right into mine. I hear music coming from out back, so I snag a drink from the fridge, then make my outside.

"What's up, man?" he asks as I walk out the sliding glass door.

"Not a whole lot. Just got some time to kill before picking up Sawyer from my parents' at four."

"He excited about Topgolf tonight?" Ryan asks.

"Yeah, you can say that again. He's been pumped since I mentioned it to him earlier this week."

"Were you trying to meet Allison early?"

"Not exactly," I tell him, pausing to take a swig of my drink. I'd call it liquid courage, but this isn't alcohol, so there's not much courage to be found in this sports drink. *"I wanted to be the one to tell you that Courtney and I have been seeing one another."*

"Ah," he says, and I can tell he's connecting the dots. *"So you're the asshole I need to read the riot act to, huh?"* He smirks and gives me a once-over.

"If you think that's truly necessary." I don't back down. He knows the kind of man I am, and that isn't the kind who plays with a woman. I'm a straight shooter when it comes to relationships. If things are working, then great, but if they aren't, then I bow out. No need to deliberately hurt the other person.

"I'm just giving you shit. I'd wondered a while ago if there might be something going on, but then I wasn't so sure. You've got my blessing, but I'll fuck you up if you hurt her. She's already been hurt enough."

"I'll help you myself if I was to ever hurt her."

"Fuck, that means that it's you I have to be thinking about with her next weekend?" He groans. *"Please don't ever give me details about y'all's escapades. I don't think I can stomach knowing that about my sister."* He mimics dry heaving, and I can't help but laugh at the antics.

"I don't kiss and tell," I say.

"Thank god," he says. I hold out a fist for him to bump, which he does. I knew he'd be cool about this, and now that it's out in the open, I want to run to Courtney, pull her into my arms, and claim her for the world to know.

We shoot the shit for a little while longer. It feels good to spend time with my best friend. We don't get enough of it during the season.

"I should get going. Sawyer has already texted to ask when I'm picking him up so we can go to Topgolf."

"Impatient kids." Ryan chuckles.

"Just wait, my man. You'll have one of your own one day, and they'll end up running everything."

"Looking forward to it," he says.

"Things getting that serious with Allison?" I ask.

"I could see it getting there. Not trying to rush anything, but she's amazing. I'm ready for her to meet those important to me."

"Happy for you, brother," I tell him as we stand and give one another a man hug. "I'll catch you in a little bit," I say before I head for my truck.

Before I pull out of the driveway, I shoot a text to Sawyer, letting him know I'm on my way to pick him up, then I hit the call button on the dash screen to call Courtney as I pull out and point my truck in the direction I need to go.

"Hello." Courtney's sweet voice fills my truck.

"Hey, beautiful. How's your afternoon going?"

"Good. I just finished getting ready after my shift. Didn't want to go out tonight smelling like burgers and fries."

"How was Jax's playdate?"

"He's been talking my ear off since I picked him up. It went really well."

"Glad he had a good time."

"What have you been up to today?" she asks.

"Just left your brother's house. We had a good talk."

"So he knows?" she asks, and I can tell she's nervous.

"Yep, and he gave us his blessing. He did threaten to kick my ass if I ever hurt you, but I'd expect nothing less. He also told me I'm not allowed to tell him about our sex life." I chuckle.

"Please tell me he didn't actually say that?" she groans.

"Maybe not those exact words, but he definitely said something about not being able to stomach any details. But just to be clear, and I told him the same thing—I don't kiss and tell. What happens between the two of us stays between the two of us."

"That makes me feel a little better." She pauses. "Oh, I got the green light to take next weekend off."

"Perfect. So that means I have you the *entire* weekend?"

"Guess so. What will we do with so much alone time?" She laughs, and I can hear the smile in her voice.

"Oh, there's plenty I plan to do to you."

"I look forward to it."

"Fucking tease," I growl. "I'm trying to drive here, woman. I don't need all the blood in my body rushing to my dick, at the moment."

"Sorry," she singsongs but also laughs her way through it.

"You're going to pay for that."

"Mm-hmm," she hums.

"Do you want me to come pick the two of you up once I leave my parents' house?" I ask as I pull into their neighborhood.

"Sure, that'll work for me."

"I'll be there in a half hour."

"Looking forward to it," she says before we disconnect the call.

I hop out of my truck and look down to make sure the hard-on isn't tenting my pants. Thankfully, it isn't, so I'm good to walk into my parents' house and pick up my son without having to conceal my situation.

"Hello," I call out as I walk inside.

"In the kitchen," my mom calls back, so I head that way. The smell of freshly baked chocolate chip cookies hits my nose a moment later, and my mouth is already watering as I enter the bright kitchen, where I find my mom and son.

"Smells wonderful in here," I say before pressing a kiss to my mom's cheek.

"Had to make some sweets for my favorite grandson."

"I'm your only grandson," Sawyer says as he rolls his eyes at her.

"Hey now, that's no way to treat your grandmother," I scold him, but there's humor in my voice as this is a normal occurrence, and it isn't something he does out of disrespect.

"Love you, Grandma," he tells her and pulls her into a hug.

"I know you do, squirt."

"I'm not a squirt anymore. I'm a peewee," he retorts.

My mom laughs at his comeback. "I wasn't referencing the level of hockey you play. It's just a term us old people use with you youngins."

"Oh," he replies.

"You ready to head out? We're going to stop and pick up Courtney and Jax on our way to Topgolf."

"That's dad's girlfriend," Sawyer tells my mom, using air quotes when he says girlfriend.

"Your girlfriend?" Mom asks, quirking a brow.

"We're talking and taking things slow," I tell her.

"Courtney, as in, Ryan's sister?"

"Yes. She moved back a few months ago with her son, Jax."

"You should bring her over for dinner some night. I'd love to see her. It's been ages."

"I'll see what I can do, but no promises for anything in the next few weeks."

"Alright, well, you kids have fun. Thanks for spending a few hours with me today," Mom tells Sawyer.

"Thanks, Grandma."

"Thanks, Mom," I say as she hands me a container of cookies to take home.

10

COURTNEY

Zack, our two boys, and I all arrive at the venue. Both boys are practically bouncing in their seats in the back, and I can't help but laugh at their enthusiasm.

"Are the two of you ready to have some fun?" Zack asks, and both boys cheer.

"Let's go, then," I say.

We make our way inside, and Zack gets us checked in. An employee shows us to our bay and gives us the rundown of how things work. Zack and Sawyer have been here before, so this isn't new to them like it is to me and Jax. I try to take in this place through his eyes, which are big as he takes everything in.

"Hi, I'm Macey, and I'll be taking care of y'all today. Can I get a round of drinks? Maybe some appetizers for everyone to share?"

"That'd be great," Zack tells her. "What do you boys want?"

"Mom, can I have a Sprite?" Jax asks.

"Yes," I tell him. "He'll have a Sprite. If you have a cup with a lid, that might be best for the safety of things getting knocked over," I tell Macey.

"Not a problem." She smiles at me as she taps at her little tablet. "What else can I get put in for you?"

I snag the menu and look it over. "I'll have a water and the spiked strawberry lemonade."

"Got it," Macey says.

"Another kids Sprite, and I'll take a Blue Moon," Zack tells her. "Do some pretzel bites and the chips and guac or queso sound good to get us started?" he asks me.

"I'm good with that."

"Did you want an order of both the guac and queso appetizers?" Macey asks.

"Why not? We've got two more coming, so I'm sure none of it will go to waste."

"Perfect. I'll get these going and be back in a few minutes with your first round of drinks. If you want to get started before the rest of your party arrives, feel free to do so. It's easy to add them once they arrive," Macey says.

"Can I go first?" Jax asks.

"Sure can," Zack tells him as he gets the game all set up on the computer. "For this first game, we'll keep it easy, just aim for any of the flags out there. Let's find a club that fits you," he tells him as he pulls out a few of the clubs from the bag an employee dropped off for kids. He finds one and is happy with how it fits Jax. "Alright, buddy, you need to stand within this box. Don't step over the line as you could fall off. Otherwise, have fun and see how far you can hit it."

I watch Jax step up and place his club next to the golf ball. He concentrates on the ball, then looks out to the open space with all the targets. He swings back and expertly hits the ball, sending it sailing into the air. It has a good arc to it, and he somehow manages to land it directly in the middle of a target.

"Yes!" He jumps in excitement. "I did it!"

"Careful, buddy, come this way," I call out to him, and he runs over to me.

"That was awesome!" Zack tells him and holds up a hand for a high-five, which Jax slaps hard.

"Was that you?" Ryan asks as he steps into our bay.

"Uncle Ryan!" Jax jumps up and runs into his arms. "Yes, that was me. Did you see it?" he asks.

"Some of it. You're a natural, my man." He ruffles the top of Jax's head.

"Nice of you to join us," Zack says as they smack hands.

"We were a little tied up." He smirks, and I don't miss the innuendo that goes right over the boys' heads.

"Ryan." Allison smacks his chest as her cheeks tint pink.

"Hi, I'm Courtney, this goon's sister." I also smack my brother's chest. "You must be Allison. It's so good to meet you." I offer a hand to her in greeting, and she accepts it.

"Nice to meet you, Courtney. I've heard so many good things about you. It's nice to finally put a face to the name, other than the pictures I've seen."

"Don't believe a word of it unless it was good, then believe that," I joke.

"I'm not going to tell her things that will scare her off," Ryan states.

"It's all been good, I promise. I was thinking that maybe we could get together, though. Maybe get to know one another a little better. I'm new to the area, so I don't have many girlfriends yet."

"I'd love that. Let's exchange numbers and we can plan something."

Macey returns for Ryan's and Allison's orders while we all enjoy talking and watching the boys finish the first game. Jax continues to impress all of us with his beginner's luck. He's got an eye for hitting the ball exactly where he wants it to go.

The second game is finally starting, and this time, we are all joining in. I grab my club and go to stand in the box. I have no clue what I'm doing, and I swing and miss the ball terribly on my first attempt.

"Need some help?" Zack asks as he comes up behind me. His arms wrap around my body, and he moves my hands on the club. My body does this strange thing, tensing but instantly relaxing in his touch. My ass presses against his crotch, and there's no missing the growl in my ear. "Woman, we're in public. You keep pressing that ass against my dick, and things won't be PG for much longer."

"I have no idea what you're talking about," I tease and lightly rub my ass across his thick cock. I have to hold back the moan I want to let escape. Teasing him is doing nothing but teasing me just as badly, and makes the wait until next weekend feel like a lifetime away.

"Just hit the damn ball," Ryan calls out.

"Bring the club back like this and straight back down," Zack instructs and helps me through the movements. The club connects with the ball, and it goes flying off the deck. It doesn't go as far as Jax's ball, but at least it hits the greens a little way away from the building. "Good job," Zack says before pressing a kiss just below my ear.

He steps back, and I instantly miss the feeling of his body pressed against mine. I follow him off the tee box and let Allison take her turn.

We have a really good time over the next couple of

hours. Eating, laughing, playing, and just getting along in general. I can see why my brother is so infatuated with Allison. She seems good for him, and I hope their relationship continues. I also look forward to getting to know her better because, like her, I don't have many girlfriends here. I might have grown up here, but my circle was small. I realize now that was mainly due to Chad and his controlling ways. I need some friends in my life, and Allison seems like a safe place to start.

11

ZACK

I walk into the practice facility feeling refreshed and ready to take on the week. We've got a quick one-night trip in the middle of the week, followed by our Friday night home game. It's not a hard schedule compared to some weeks.

As I walk down the hall, one of our trainers, Whitney, is standing in the doorway to a treatment room. The man she's talking to has his back to me, and I don't recognize him from this angle.

"Hey, Whit," I greet her as I walk by.

"Zack, wait up a second," she calls out. "Have you met Camden yet?" I turn around and realize she's talking to Camden Rowe. He must have made it into town over the weekend.

"Hey, man. Nice to have you join us. Was a little shocked you left San Fran."

"Nice to see you." He accepts my outstretched hand as we shake. "Wasn't on my radar, either, but you know how the business works."

"Don't I," I agree. I've had my share of trade deadline shocks in my career. I've been the guy being sent to a new team three times in six years. I'm glad that can no longer happen unless I'm the one to request it. "It's good to have you here. I'm sure you'll fit right in. We've got a good group of guys in the locker room."

"Looking forward to it. At the end of the day, all I want to do is play hockey."

"Amen to that. You got any kids? Girlfriend or wife?" I ask.

"None of the above," he says as his eyes flash over to Whitney.

"Let's plan to grab a beer or dinner on the road this week," I suggest.

"I'd like that. Thanks, man." He claps me on the shoulder.

"You free in half an hour or so?" I ask Whitney.

"You need that hip stretched?" she asks. I can already see her eyes roaming my body but not in a flirty way. In a professional trainer way as she takes in my stance. I swear she can see through us when we try to hide injuries.

"That hip flexor still tight?" she asks.

ZACK

"Yes," I admit. No sense in lying to her, or else she'll torture me when she stretches me out.

"I'll come get you when I'm ready. I have a little more to go over with Camden," she says. Whenever we get a new guy, the training staff likes to go over a bunch of things with them. From their pre-game routine to nutritional preferences. It's their job to keep us healthy and on the ice playing. And in the unfortunate times when we're hurt and can't play, they get us back on the ice when it's time.

"Sounds good. You know where to find me," I tell her as I leave the two of them and head into the locker room.

I fist-bump Easton when I walk past him. He's already in his compression clothes, ready to start some pre-practice off-ice warm-ups. "Did you meet Camden?" he asks as I take a seat and start to strip.

"Yeah, he was talking to Whitney when I walked in."

"Nice guy. I think he'll fit in well."

"Yep," I say as I pull on my compression shorts. I adjust the cup in the pocket, making sure it is sitting correctly to protect the important parts.

The next few hours fly by, which is usually a good sign of a productive practice. I feel good. We all gelled well together with the adjustment of our lines with a new guy being inserted. I'm sure Coach will try a few more line combinations to see what one works best, but it won't shock me if Camden ends up as a winger on our second line.

I TAKE A SEAT AT ONE OF THE SMALL TABLES IN THE hotel bar. A few of my teammates have gathered around at the other tables as they all wait on drinks from the bar. We've had an easy travel day and arrived in St. Louis this afternoon. We had a team dinner before being given the rest of the night as a free one. Coach trusts that we won't be out all night partying it up, especially with an important game on the line tomorrow night. We're currently in second place in our division, but we still have a ways to go before securing our place in the playoffs. We need to keep winning to make that happen.

Camden takes a seat in the chair across from me. He's got a beer glass in one hand as he sits down.

"Smart man," I tell him as I continue to wait for the one I ordered ten minutes ago.

"I got here before the rush and was just chatting with Graham and Kaden over at the other end of the bar."

"Gotcha," I say as the frazzled server stops at the table and sets down my beer. "Thanks," I tell her.

"Did you have anything else?" she asks.

"Nope, this was all."

"Great. Just flag me down if you need anything else," she says. They must not have thought the entire team would come here tonight, as there's only the one server and bartender on right now. Needless to say, none of us are in a rush or worried.

"Will do. You're doing a great job," I assure her.

"Thanks, I'm trying. It's only my third shift, so I'm still learning the ropes." I think of Courtney and how it must have been for her when she started working as a server. People can be such assholes to servers when things aren't coming out as quickly as they think they should be.

"My girlfriend is a part-time server, so I understand the stress," I say, hoping it will help her nerves.

"She's lucky to have you," she says before walking away.

"It's the opposite," I start to say, but she's too far away to hear me in the noisy bar. The word must have gotten out that we're here as people start to pour in, making the place that much more packed and busy.

"Want to head up to the lounge?" I ask Camden. We have a reserved lounge for the team.

"Yeah, I'm ready to get out of this place," he says as he looks around at the packed room. We both take our drinks and make our way out. I hit the button of the elevator. Once inside, I slide my room key along the sensor that allows me to select the floor the lounge is on.

"How long were you in San Francisco?" I ask as we ride up.

"Went there two seasons ago during the offseason."

"Nice place they built out there."

"Yeah, they spared no expense when they were building. Nathan, the owner, wanted the place to have all the newest and best things available to his team."

"How much of a surprise was it for you to come here?" I ask.

"A little, but my agent called me early last week and said he'd gotten word that there was a possibility. It just sucks, as I was around my family. My sister is married to Blake Watson."

"The goalie?" I ask.

"The one and only. That was a trip to get my head wrapped around." He laughs. "They met randomly one weekend during the summer in Vegas. He was there for his brother's bachelor party weekend, and she was there for her best friend's bachelorette party weekend. A month later, she realized she was pregnant from the one-night stand but had no clue who he was. Fast-forward a few months, she transfers to San Fran to be near me and comes to a game. They see one another after the game and the rest is history. They're happily married and have another kid on the way. I didn't take the news that he was the one to knock my sister up very well, but once I got over the shock, everything was smooth sailing after that."

"Damn, that's quite the story."

"Yeah. But they're happy, so who am I to stand in their way?"

"I'm dating my best friend's little sister, so I get it. He was cool with it. We're still new. She got out of a long relationship only a few months ago that wasn't a good one, so we're taking things slow for her sake. You ready to settle down?"

"Not really looking, but also not *not* looking, if that makes sense."

"Right there with you, man. That's how it happened for Courtney and me. She moved back, we ran into one another, and it was this instant pull. I just had to be around her as much as possible. Which can be a bitch between my schedule and the fact we're both single parents. She's on her own, except for her brother and parents' help. I, at least, have my ex and parents around."

"How old is your kid?" he asks.

"Sawyer is ten going on twenty-five, I swear. He's a

good kid. Got an ego the size of Texas, but he's a good kid."

"Nice. He plays, then?"

"Oh yes. He's doing his best to get better than me." I chuckle. "If he keeps it up, the little shit will pass me by with his skills. Not that I'll ever admit that to him." I take a swig of my beer as we shoot the shit.

"Kids, they keep you humble, that's for sure."

"No shit."

A handful of the other guys end up joining us in the lounge. The bar was getting a little too rowdy for their liking.

It's getting late, and I know my alarm will go off early, so I call it a night and head for my room. I pull out my cell and shoot Courtney a text, hoping I've caught her before she's gone to bed for the night.

ZACK

You still awake?

No bubbles pop up right away, so I slide my phone back into my pocket as I tap my room key over the sensor and the green light flashes, letting me know the lock is open. I push the door and step inside the quiet room. I stop in the bathroom, taking a piss before I wash my hands, then brush my teeth before bed. Walking into the main part of the room, I strip down to my boxers, then slide under the sheet. I grab my phone from where I'd tossed it on the bed and see Courtney replied.

> **COURTNEY**
>
> Yes, just was reading before falling asleep. How was your team dinner?

I want to see her face, so rather than replying via text, I hit the FaceTime button and call her. The call connects and I get a dimly lit view of her. "Hold on, let me turn on my lamp," she says before stretching and turning it on. The light brings her into view so much better.

"How was your day?" I ask just as she starts taking.

"How was your dinner?"

"You go first," I say.

"It was okay."

"Just okay?" I say, worried something happened.

"Erin called. Chad's attorney replied and is demanding a hearing. He does't want to agree to the terms we've offered. Erin thinks we should go to court. She found out some information on him that I wasn't aware of that she thinks will work in our favor."

"So what are you going to do?" I ask.

"I can only trust that she knows best. I'm just worried, ya know? What happens if I lose full custody?" A tear runs down her cheek and I wish I was there to hold her and wipe them from her eyes.

"Then we fight it. But I have a good feeling that isn't going to happen. You have all the proof showing that you've always been Jax's primary care giver. I'm not one to advocate for stripping a parent of their kids, but when the situation calls for it, then go for it."

"I'm just nervous, but enough about that tonight. I need to get my mind off it, so tell me how your team dinner was," she says, so I do.

"It was a good, normal time. I got to know Camden a little better. Trying to make him feel welcomed into the group."

"That's nice of you."

"Yeah, I've been in his shoes before. It always takes a few weeks to really feel part of a new team, especially mid-season when everyone else has been together for the majority of the season."

"Are you ready for the game tomorrow night?" she asks.

"Yep, feeling really good. Practice has been good this week. We're all gelling well."

"That's good. Jax and I are going to watch until bedtime."

"I'll do my best to score a goal for the two of you." I wink into the camera.

"Will you now?" She smiles back. "Maybe if you score a goal on the ice, I'll let you score one off."

"Promise?" My voice is husky as I think about sinking into her body.

"How long until Friday night?" she asks.

"Too damn long," I tell her honestly. It's only Tuesday, so we've got a way to go between now and our weekend together. I glance at the clock and see that it's almost midnight. "I should let you get to sleep," I say as Courtney covers a yawn.

"Yeah, I'm having a hard time keeping my eyes open. I'll talk to you tomorrow, okay?"

"Sweet dreams, sweetheart. Text or call when you can. We'll be headed to the rink around four, so it will be hit or miss after that until the game is over."

"Okay. Good night, Zack," she says, and we disconnect the call.

I plug my phone in, then shut off the lights and roll over, doing my best to fall asleep.

12

COURTNEY

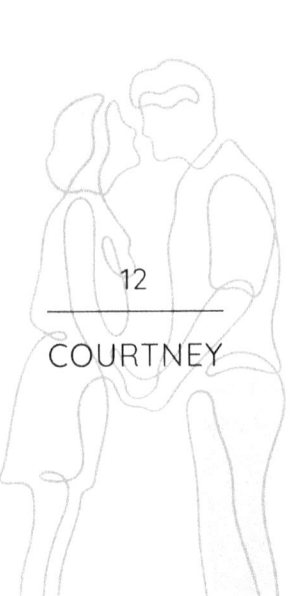

I STAND IN THE FAMILY SECTION OF THE RINK, waiting on Zack to come out of the locker room. My nerves are on high alert after the game the guys just played. That, coupled with what's about to come for the rest of the weekend, and I swear I could catch something on fire with the electricity flowing through my veins.

The door opens and I hold my breath, waiting to see who emerges. I blow my breath out when it isn't him. The guy walks straight past the small group of people waiting, mostly wives and girlfriends. A few of the women have kids with them. The door opens again, and a few of them trickle out this time, Zack being one of them. He shoots me a wink as he walks over to me, stopping inches from me. "Hi, sweetheart," he greets, leaning in and pressing a kiss to the corner of my mouth. "Ready to get out of here?"

"Yes," I breathily answer.

He slips my hand into his and links our fingers together. The butterflies that have taken up a home in my stomach are in full flutter mode as we walk out of the rink, hand in hand.

"You had a great game tonight," I tell him as we walk to his truck.

"I promised you a goal, and I deliver on my promises," he states. The deep timbre of his voice sends chills down my spine and right to my core that is more than ready for him.

I giggle—fucking giggle like I'm a schoolgirl—at his words. When we make it to his truck, before he reaches around me to open the door, he presses me up against it and captures my lips with his own.

I fist his dress shirt, holding him close as we kiss against his truck.

"Get a room," someone calls out before whistling as they walk past.

"Fuck off," Zack calls back as he chuckles. "Let's get out of here. I need you naked sooner rather than later."

The drive to Zack's place feels like it only takes seconds. We don't talk much, but the silent conversation between us is loud in my mind. The way his hand cups my thigh and the slight touch of his thumb as it moves back and forth across my sensitive skin have my body ready to combust. I know I'm going to embarrass myself with how quickly I come once we're naked and in bed together.

Zack pulls into his garage and shuts off the truck. "Are you okay?" he asks. "Awfully quiet."

"I'm great, just the anticipation of tonight."

He reaches over and turns my chin so I'm looking at him. His eyes are so caring, and I could easily get lost in them if I don't look away. "We can take things slow. If all you want to do is cuddle fully clothed, then that's what we'll do," he says, and I know he'd stick to that if that's what I wanted.

"I'm good. Can we go inside? I'd like to kiss you some more."

He reaches over and opens the driver's door and slips out of the truck. I follow suit from the passenger side. We meet at the front of the truck. He leans down and plants a kiss on my lips but quickly pulls away. He leads me inside his house. It feels so different to be walking in, knowing that we're all alone. No kids to interrupt. Nothing holding us back except our own self-doubts.

"Can I get you anything? A drink? Some food?" Zack offers.

"I'm good. I had dinner at the rink. I do, however, need to use the restroom. The pop I had was huge."

"Of course. You know where it is down the hall," Zack says, and I turn for the hallway. After closing the door, I lean against it for a second, sucking in a deep breath. I'm so ready for this weekend, but now that it's here, the nerves are high. We had that one night that was so spontaneous, but there's something about knowing that nothing stands between us and sex. Sex changes things—sometimes for the better, and sometimes for the worse.

I push off the door and quickly do my business. I'm washing my hands when there's a soft knock on the door. *"You okay in there?"* Zack asks.

I open the door and give him a smile. *"Yep, all done."*

"Let me see your shirt," Zack says. He reaches for the jean jacket I had on over the shirt and pulls the sides away so he can see the entire design. I'd been scrolling through Instagram a couple of weeks ago when I saw a wife from another player's pictures. She'd tagged the girl who made some custom shirts, and I reached out to see how much they were. She had lots of options to pick from, so I splurged and ordered one. I hadn't told Zack about it and wanted to surprise him with it. It has the team's logo in a graffiti style, along with Zack's number hidden all within the design. On the back, it has his last name across the top and his number in a large matching font.

"Where'd you get this?" he asks, his eyes filled with awe.

"I special ordered it. Want to see the back?" I ask. He helps take off my jacket, and I spin around, showing him the back.

"Seeing my name and number on your back is the sexiest thing you could have worn tonight," he says as he closes the space between us and presses his front to my back. He slides my hair off my neck, and his lips find the open space.

I tilt my head, giving him better access, so he nibbles his way to my ear. "Feel what you do to me?" he asks as his hard cock presses against my ass.

"Yes," I moan as he slips a hand under my shirt and slides it up to cup my breast. He tugs my bra cup down and rolls my nipple between his fingers. We stay there in the hallway, him kissing my neck and playing with my nipple for a minute or two.

I stop his torment and turn in his arms to face him. Zack moves his hands to my ass and cups my cheeks as he holds me tightly against his body. I kiss him hard but pull back before he can deepen the kiss any further. "Take me to your bedroom," I instruct.

I'm caught off guard when he bends me backward and plants a kiss on my lips, then just as quickly pulls away and swoops me up into his arms. He's carrying me down the hall the next moment and into his bedroom, not stopping until he sets me on the foot of the bed. "Any more commands?" he asks.

I think for a few seconds, and an idea strikes me. I stand and move to face him, then drop to my knees. I've thought about this very moment for weeks. I've wanted to repay the sexual favor he gave me. Not that I feel like it's repayment, but it's something I've wanted to give him. I reach forward and undo his belt. My movements are slow and calculated. The whoosh his belt makes as it slips through the buckle, followed by the sound his zipper makes as it slides down the metal teeth. I tug his slacks down, taking his black boxer briefs with me. His hard cock springs free, almost slapping me in the face with how close I am to him. I tug his clothes until they're down around his ankles. He must have taken his shoes off while I was in the bathroom, as they are no longer on his feet. He quickly steps out of the pants and underwear. I reach forward and grip his hard cock. The heat from it is almost scorching, and he hisses at the contact. "Too much?" I ask and release my grip.

"No, your touch has me almost ready to blow."

I smile up at him as seductively as I can. Zack collects my hair, holding it out of my face as I lean forward and suck the head of his cock between my lips. I swirl my tongue around his crown as his fist tightens in my hair. His other hand works at the buttons of his dress shirt until it is fully open.

"Fuuuuuck," he growls. "Your mouth feels fucking fantastic on my cock."

I slide my fist down his shaft as I take more of it into my mouth, my lips stretching as I do. His tip hits the back of my throat, and I have to breathe through my nose so I don't gag on it. I pull back, then slide it right back in.

The words falling from Zack's mouth are inaudible but tell me he's enjoying this all the same. I continue to bob up and down, taking him to the back of my throat, then all the way out to his crown. After a few times, I remove him from my mouth completely but continue to slide my hand up and down his shaft, never letting up on the pressure. "Are you coming in my mouth tonight?" I ask.

"Hell no, you're coming first," he says before reaching down and sliding his hands under my arms and hauling me up. "I'll come down your throat another time," he says before kissing me hard.

We break apart long enough to fully strip out of our clothes. Once we're both naked, he lays me back on the king-size bed and follows me down. His mouth finds mine once again, and we become a tangled mix of limbs. Like last time, it's as if he's mapping my body with his fingers and lips. As he slips down, I slide up the bed until we're both on it, with him between my legs. "Prop yourself up and watch as I devour this pussy." He flicks his tongue down my center, and I about come off the bed in anticipation. "Just as good as I remember," he says before diving in for more. My clit is already pulsing when his tongue makes contact.

"Zack!" I scream his name. I don't hold back as I let my body just enjoy the intense pleasure. I let myself fall apart as he brings me to the edge, then backs off, only to bring me right back to the edge and finally cresting over. I see stars and feel my body go limp as he slides up, dropping kisses on the way. I have no idea what he's doing as I bask in the feeling, but I can feel him moving around for a few moments before he joins me, pulling me into his side.

We lay that way for a few minutes, the stars finally disappearing as our surroundings return. "Ready for more?" he asks.

"I'm ready for anything with you," I confess. He rolls me under him and kisses me tenderly. I can feel his hard cock throbbing against my leg. I look down when he breaks the kiss and he grips his shaft. He's already covered it with a condom. He slides his tip through my folds, teasing my very tender clit a few times before bringing it back down to my entrance.

He captures my mouth as he thrusts inside me, swallowing my gasp of pleasure as he stretches me to take him fully. He stills once fully seated. "You okay?" he asks against my lips.

"I'm perfect," I tell him, and he slowly thrusts. My body is on such high alert, it isn't going to take much before I'm coming again. As his rhythm increases, I move my mouth to his neck and scream my pleasure into the crook as he takes me over the edge, not slowing down as my body clenches around his shaft.

"You're beautiful when you come. That's it, baby. Come on that cock as I fuck you hard." His words spur me on.

"I'm coming again," I cry out.

"Fuck, fuck, fuck," he chants as he thrusts through my body, clenching him like a vise grip, milking his own release out of him. He collapses on top of me, pinning me to the bed as he enjoys the endorphin ride.

We stay that way for a few minutes, our bodies relaxed and in a blissed state of mutual satisfaction. Zack eventually pushes up some, taking his weight off me. "Sorry about pinning you to the bed. I didn't hurt you, did I?" he asks as he rolls over and takes me with him.

"I'm perfectly fine," I assure him. I lay my head on his chest and the sound of his heart beating almost lulls me to sleep as we both lay there enjoying the peacefulness while in one another's arms.

"I should take care of the condom," he finally says, his voice a little groggy.

"I need to clean up, as well," I tell him as we both slip apart and out of the bed. He leads me into the en suite bathroom. He grabs some toilet paper and removes the condom, then tosses it into the trash.

"Do you want to shower or take a bath before bed?" he asks.

"No, but I'll definitely take you up on that offer in the morning."

"Okay. Are you hungry? I've worked up an appetite."

"I suppose I could go for a snack. What do you have?" I ask.

"Let me go check," he offers before stepping out of the bathroom and leaving me to myself for a few minutes. I quickly pee, then rinse my mouth out with some water, then find his mouthwash and swish some of that around.

I head back into the bedroom and find my panties, then go into his closet to see if I can find a T-shirt to borrow. The first drawer I open is the jackpot, and I grab the one on top, pulling it over my head. The hem of it goes halfway down my thighs it's so big. But it smells like him, so I pull the fabric to my nose and take a deep breath. I slip out of the bedroom and make my way down to the kitchen, where Zack stands in nothing but his boxer briefs at the kitchen counter, assembling a tray with what looks like a few kinds of cheese, meats, crackers, and fruit.

"Hey, gorgeous." He smiles at me. "Wasn't sure what you were hungry for, so I made us a little bit of everything easy to eat."

"Looks fantastic. Can I help at all?" I offer.

"Just stand there looking like my next meal." He smirks, and it just about has my panties melting off.

"I hope you don't mind that I stole one of your T-shirts from the drawer in your closet."

"It looks good on you." He smiles and holds up the tray he's finished assembling. It doesn't look fancy, but I'm not complaining. "Let's go back to bed. We can relax and eat," Zack suggests before placing a chaste kiss on my lips.

"Do you want me to grab anything?"

"I'll take a water from the fridge, grab whatever you want."

I open the fridge and find it well stocked with waters, electrolyte drinks, cans of soda, and a few beers. I snag two bottles of water and follow Zack back to the bedroom.

We sit up in bed with the sheets pulled up to our laps. Zack places the tray of food in front of us so we can sit side by side. He feeds me a bite, and I do the same, stopping for kisses occasionally. Once we've finished eating, he takes the tray back down to the kitchen, then returns and slides right back into bed next to me. Zack clicks off the lamp on his side of the bed, leaving only the moon shining in from outside to provide any light. We both settle in, and he pulls me closer to his side. I rest my head in the crook of his arm and relax in the comfort of them.

"You fit perfectly here," Zack says, his voice raspy with sleep.

"I could get used to being right here. The security of your arms around me while I sleep."

"Then stay," he says before we drift off to sleep.

13

ZACK

I wake up, a little confused, at first, as to where I am. It takes a minute for my eyes to adjust to the room, remembering I'm in my own bed and that Courtney is curled up next to me. We've rolled onto our sides, with me spooned around her sexy body. I slide my hand up from her belly and cup her breast. Her nipples are already hardened peaks.

"Mhmm, good morning, sweetheart," I whisper into her ear as her ass rubs against my cock. There are only two very thin layers of fabric between us, layers that won't be hard to shed before I can sink back inside her perfect body.

"Mornin'." She sighs as I slide my hand down and under the elastic of her panties. I find her wet and ready for me. "Zack," she says on a gasp as I push two fingers inside her pussy. Courtney rolls toward me, and I capture her mouth in a searing kiss. My tongue tangles with hers as I slide my fingers in and out of her center and rub circles with my thumb around her clit.

I break the kiss, not wanting to miss her falling with just the touch of my hand. "That's it, beautiful. Come for me," I whisper into her skin. I add more pressure to her clit and switch my movements to a come-hither motion, finding her G-spot. It isn't long before she falls over the edge.

"What a way to wake up," Courtney says a few minutes later.

"I agree. Best morning ever." I press a kiss to her lips. "How about some breakfast?"

"Yes, I'm starving."

"Do you want to go out or stay in and cook?" I ask.

"I'm fine with either."

"How about a shower, and then we can go out? I think there's a place not far with a big weekend brunch."

"Perfect. Will you shower with me?"

"Of course, let's go."

It's amazing how easily we are able to adjust to being together, from the ease of showering together to getting ready for the day. I picked up a weekend bag from Courtney to bring to my house earlier in the week since she was coming home with me last night and wouldn't be able to bring it to the rink with her. I watch as she gets ready while I brush my teeth, my eyes falling to the bathroom counter where her stuff is all laid out. I like seeing it like that, her in my space, our things intermixed. My mind flips forward—months, maybe years down the road—and I can picture every morning just like this one, nights just like last night, where we fall asleep wrapped up in each other. The ease that has come from this relationship has made me believe in love and happily ever after once again.

We find the restaurant, and thankfully, the wait for a table isn't super long. We are shown to one that's tucked along the windows. The sun is shining bright, and the sky is nice and blue today without a cloud in it.

"Welcome. Can I interest either of you in our bottomless mimosas today?"

"Not for me. Sweetheart, do you want one?" I ask Courtney.

"No, thank you, but I will take a glass of your fresh-squeezed orange juice," she tells the server.

"I'll have the same, please."

"Did you want larges for those?" she asks.

"Yes, please," I answer for both of us.

"Perfect, I'll get those right out to you. If you want to head up to the buffet, you'll find all of our signature dishes. There's also a made-to-order egg station, waffles, and pancakes."

"Yum, I'm so hungry, and all of that sounds amazing," Courtney says.

As soon as our server leaves the table, we head to the buffet, both filling our plates full with all they have to offer. When we make it back to our table, our server has dropped off our drinks.

"Oh my god," Courtney moans after swallowing a bite. "I think this is the best eggs Benedict I've ever had. Want to try a bite?" She offers me her fork with a bite on the end.

"I'm tempted, but I'll have to pass. I'm not a fan of hollandaise sauce."

She pops the bite into her mouth, and I've never been more jealous of a fork in my life. We take our time enjoying the kid-free breakfast and one another's company.

"What should we go do now?" I ask as we walk out to the parking lot, hand in hand.

"I'm open to whatever you want to do. The only thing I had on my calendar for today was spending it with you," Courtney says. I stop us in front of my truck and pull her into a kiss. I keep it tame since we are in public.

"Do you want to go shopping?" I ask.

"We can. Is there something that you need?"

"No, I just want to take you. Spoil you today. Maybe stop at a lingerie store and buy something for tonight." I lean in and kiss her neck, just below her ear.

"Hmm," she hums. "I like that idea. If you're a good boy, I'll even let you in the dressing room while I try things on."

I step back and drag her over to the passenger door, opening it as soon as the locks click.

Courtney laughs. "Someone's in a hurry."

"The thought of you modeling lingerie? Yes please." I help her up into the truck. I quickly make my way around the front and hop into the driver's seat. I pull out and drive straight to the large mall filled with all sorts of stores.

We walk around the busy mall, checking out stores as they call to us. "We should go get pedicures," Courtney suggests as we walk past a nail place.

"If that's what you want to do, we can," I tell her. It isn't something I'd normally do, but today is all about new beginnings, so what the hell.

We walk into the salon and are greeted by one of the workers who leads us to two empty large massage chairs. He starts filling the basins with water and instructs us to take a seat and get comfortable. Another employee brings over a few books filled with color options for Courtney to pick from. She mulls over all the color options, finally picking a bright pink one.

"What pedicure would you like?" the lady asks. She hands me a laminated piece of paper with all their options explained.

"We'll both do the ultimate," I tell her, picking the most expensive option on the menu.

"I'd have been fine with a basic," Courtney says once the employee walks away.

"Let me spoil you today," I tell her.

"Thank you," she concedes and smiles at me.

Two employees return with a tray filled with different products. I'm assuming they're the different things they'll use for our pedicures. I lower my feet into the hot water and suck in a quick breath as I adjust to the temperature of the water.

"Aw, is it too hot for you?" Courtney teases. She has no issues lowering her feet into the basin of her chair.

"I like my skin, thank-you-very-much."

"Don't be a baby. How ticklish are your feet?" she asks, a grin on her face.

"Oh shit," I groan as the lady adds something to the water. Courtney is full-on giggling next to me as I look distraught.

"You'll be fine. I'll hold your hand, if needed," she offers through her laughter.

"Woman." I try to sound harsh, but it comes out pretty weak. "I'll get you later," I warn.

"Promise?"

I don't answer her with spoken words, but the way I devour her with my eyes tells her how much of a promise I've just made.

The next hour passes with a lot of squirming. I didn't realize how ticklish my feet were until I got this pedicure. The massage portion feels great, but I could have done without the scrubby thing they used on the bottom of my feet. I had a hard time not giggling like a freaking schoolgirl.

Courtney gets her toes painted and even a design added to her big toes. While she waits for the paint to fully dry, I take care of paying. Once she can put her shoes back on, we head back into the mall. We slowly make our way in and out of more stores. I've realized just how much Courtney loves to stop and smell candles as she looks at things. I swear she's stopped to smell them in every store that has them. "Do you want that one?" I ask.

"No, I never burn them. I'm always afraid I'll forget about it or that Jax would accidentally get hurt by them. I just love stopping to smell them," she says.

"My mom has those little wax melting pots in her house. Says they are safer than an open flame."

"I've seen them, but they just have never been

within my budget." I hate that she's always had to pinch her pennies. It really brings into perspective how lucky I am, which isn't something I like to take for granted.

We finally make it into one of the department stores, and over to the lingerie department. Courtney looks all through the racks, and I just stand back and observe her. Memorizing what items she's drawn to. She holds up a few items for my reaction. "I like whatever you will feel the most comfortable and sexy in."

"What's your favorite color?"

"On you?" I ask for clarification.

"Sure," she says as she looks through a rack of bras.

"Any color of the rainbow," I say.

Her eyes flick to mine. "Ha ha, very funny."

"I'm serious. Whatever color you have on at the moment is my favorite."

She grabs a few things, and I snag another few, and we go in search of a dressing room. "Shh, you have to stay quiet," she warns as we enter the little room and close the door. I take a seat on the only chair and get ready for the show.

"Close your eyes," Courtney instructs as she strips out of her clothes.

"That wasn't part of the deal," I whine.

"Do it, or I'll make you wait outside," she warns.

I try to fight it, but eventually close my eyes. With

my eyes closed, my other senses intensify, and I can hear every movement she makes, every rustle of fabric as she removes clothes and puts others on.

"Okay, open," she says, and I do just that. My eyes fly open, and I take her in, standing a few feet from me. The little nighty she put on first is like wrapping paper. She's all tied up with a bow for me to remove to get my prize. "What do you think?" she asks, and I realize my silence has her worried.

I immediately get to my feet and close the distance between us to pull her into my arms. "You made me speechless. I thought I was looking at a gift," I tell her. "Anything you put on will be gorgeous, just like you." I bring my lips to hers and do my best to keep it light. I break our connection. "What's next?" I say before stepping back and taking a seat on the chair.

Courtney tries on the other things, having me close my eyes with each one until she has it on and can show me. Nothing she tries on looks bad. It's like it was all made to showcase her in the best possible ways. She picks out her favorite pieces, and we head back out into the store. I need some new dress shoes, so after a quick stop in the men's shoe department, we check out and head back into the mall.

"Are you hungry?" Courtney asks as we walk past the food court.

"Not really, are you?"

"No, brunch was so much. I just wasn't sure about you since it's been a few hours already."

"I'll be good until dinner," I assure her. "Are you ready to get out of here?"

"I think so. We've walked the entire mall, so unless you want to go back and look at something, I'm good."

We head for my truck, and on our way, her phone rings. "Hello," she says as she puts the phone to her ear.

I look over to make sure everything is okay, and the smile that lights up her face answers my question.

"Wow, that sounds so fun! I miss you, too," she says, and I figure she's talking to Jax.

We find the truck, and after helping Courtney get into the passenger side, I hop into the driver's side. She's put the call on speaker, so I can now hear everything Jax is telling her about his day with Ryan.

"We went mini golfing again, and I beat Uncle Ryan big time, Mommy. Then, we went out for ice cream, and then we went to Target, and he let me pick out any toy I wanted."

"Wow, sounds like Uncle Ryan is spoiling you big time."

"Damn straight," he says in the background. "Best perk of being the favorite uncle."

"What else do the two of you have planned for today?" Courtney asks.

"We're picking up takeout and then having a movie night," Ryan answers.

"Fun!" Courtney says.

"Mommy, are you with Zack?" Jax asks.

She looks up at me, and I give her a slight nod. "Yes, honey," she says.

"I like him, Mommy."

"I like him, too," she says with a huge smile.

"Gotta go, love you!" Jax calls out before the call ends.

"Love you, too," Courtney says to the phone, even though the call has already ended.

"Well, that went well," I muse.

"Guess it did." She chuckles. "Now, where were we?"

"Headed back to my place. Unless you wanted to stop somewhere else?" I ask before I pull out of the parking spot.

"Not that I can think of."

We're lying on the couch, supposedly watching the movie playing, but I don't think either of us are paying any attention to it. My attention is fully on Courtney as she fidgets next to me as we're spread out on the couch.

"What's wrong?"

Courtney rolls so she's facing me as we lie on the couch. "Just thinking about everything. Us, the boys, my meeting with Erin this week."

"What's bothering you the most?" I tuck a lock of hair behind her ear, hoping my touch will help calm her mind.

"Probably the meeting with Erin. It's the whole unknown that comes with that."

"I can understand how that could be stressful."

"Can I ask you something?"

"Anything, sweetheart."

"Did you and Emerson ever fight over your custody agreement, or was it all easygoing?"

"For the most part, it was easy. We were young when we had him. We tried for a couple of years, but we just weren't meant to be together as a couple. I was playing in another state, and it was hard for me to get back here to see them often. She wanted to stay here where she had family to help. That's when I hired Erin and had her draw up everything. We went back and forth a few times, hammering out all the little details, before we were both happy with everything. Once I signed here, we made a few changes to it, but nothing major. And now that Sawyer is a little older, we kind of let him lead things. When I'm home and available, he comes here as much as possible. In the offseason, I have him a lot more. I pay for all of his hockey stuff, as well as child support."

"I don't think Chad ever really wanted to have kids. He was always so absent and didn't ever deal with Jax when he was a baby. Chad hated when he'd cry or make a lot of noise. I got really acquainted with taking him to the park or the mall play places because they were free and, in the summer, air-conditioned. I'm just so stumped as to why he's all of a sudden fighting so hard for custody."

"Probably to hurt you. He knows that the last thing you would give up is Jax. Asshole people use their kids as pawns, especially in custody battles. I'm sorry you're going through this, but just know I'll be right here every step of the way. However you need me to be."

"I can't thank you enough for all you've done already."

"Now, what else was on your mind? You said us. What about us?"

"The past twenty-four hours have felt like such a fairy tale. How do we leave this bubble tomorrow and live outside of it?"

"Why do we need to leave the bubble?" I ask, honestly wanting to know her reasoning.

"How can we not? I can't pawn my kid off on my

brother all the time. Sawyer will be back, and we've both got work. The list of reasons goes on."

"Honey, that's just our lives. We can still be us with all of that going on. I love spending time with Jax. If that means I come to your place because that's where he's most comfortable, then so be it. If he'd be okay here, then hell, we can set up one of the guest rooms for him. I know we said we'd take things slow, but I don't know if I can go slow after this weekend. I want to be with you. No, scratch that. I need to be with you like I need air to breathe."

"I'm not ready to move in together, if that's what you're hinting at."

"I wasn't, but it isn't a bad idea." I pause, letting my words sink in. "When you're ready." I laugh when she pokes me in the ribs. "You are so easy to rile up."

"I should have known you'd be a jokester."

"All jokes aside, I don't think we should hide our relationship. Let it be out in the open. We can tell the boys. I'm not against us doing things apart. I'll need to spend time with Sawyer, as you need time with Jax, but I'd also like to try to incorporate that time together. Would you be okay with that?"

"Are you sure you're real?" Courtney asks.

"Does this feel fake to you?" I lean in and kiss her, pulling her flush against me. My cock swells in the basketball shorts I changed into after dinner and presses into her abdomen.

"Definitely not fake," she says against my lips once we break apart.

Courtney pulls in a deep breath, slowly letting it out before she replies, "Yes." That's the only answer I needed to hear. I haul us both up off the couch and carry her down the hall to the bedroom, where I strip us both bare and show her just how good we can be together.

14

COURTNEY

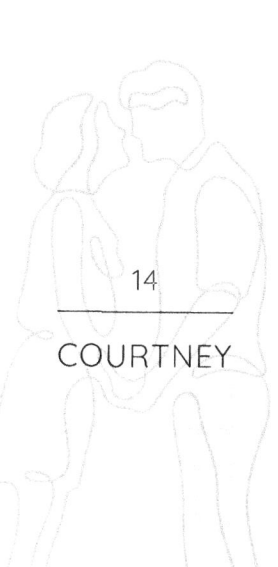

I sit in a conference room in Erin's office, waiting for her to join me. My nerves are on high alert as the minutes tick past. Her assistant assured me she'd be right in. She was just finishing up a phone call when I arrived.

"Hello," Erin says as she breezes through the door a few minutes later. "Sorry to keep you waiting, but that call had to do with your case, so I needed to finish it before meeting with you."

"Everything okay?" I ask nervously.

"It will be." Erin smiles at me from across the table where she's taken a seat. She opens the file folder she carried in with her and shuffles some papers around before turning a stack of them and placing them in front of me.

"Were you aware that Mr. Whittle was arrested a few weeks ago for drug possession?" Erin asks.

"He was what?!" I almost screech, but compose myself slightly.

"I didn't think so. He's been charged with possession, intent to distribute, and crossing state lines, among some other charges. The feds are also involved. They believe he's involved with a larger ring."

"Please tell me this helps our case for denying him custody," I ask her, dumbfounded by this news.

"It does. I already sent a motion to the judge to throw out his petition and to sign ours based on the new details of Mr. Whittle's current legal situation. I haven't gone as far as to request his parental rights be stripped, as that's extreme. Judges usually aren't too keen on doing that as a first step, but we can keep it in our wheelhouse should things with his current situation get even worse."

"I'm in shock. Do you know how long it will take for the judge to make a decision?"

"It should be within the next couple of days. The motion I filed was an emergency injunction, so they make those a priority. I've asked for full legal and physical custody. If visitation is awarded, I've asked that it be supervised and only at a location within twenty-five miles from your residence."

"And what about child support?" I ask.

"That is determined by the state. He's been served with paperwork to submit proof of his current income, along with copies of last year's tax return. The state has a formula on how they calculate what he will be required to pay."

"And if he ends up in jail because of these charges?" I ask.

"Then he'll become delinquent, and the amount will just accumulate. Whenever he'd get out and could start working, money would be garnished to start paying it."

"I'm still so shocked about today's revelation, but also not surprised, either. He was always so secretive, and I thought it was just that he was cheating on me. Turns out it was even worse; he was selling drugs!"

"Don't blame yourself for any of his behavior. He knew right from wrong and made his decisions."

"I can't thank you enough for all the work you've done on my case."

"That's what I'm here for. Once I get word from the judge, I'll call you with the updates."

"And what happens after that?"

"If he grants our request, that will be the order until a new one is filed. If Mr. Whittle never files for a new one, then nothing has to change."

"It can really be that simple?"

"It can, but I also want you to know that he could

still fight it, even with his current charges. Just because he's facing jail time doesn't mean he can't also be fighting for custody. Until he's found guilty, the courts could look beyond that or make a temporary order until there's an outcome in that criminal case."

"Okay."

"On a more personal note, you've got a good thing going with Zack. I've had the pleasure of getting to know him over the years, first as a client and then as one of my husband's teammates."

"I've known him pretty much my entire life. I just never thought I'd be where I am now. He was always just my older brother's best friend, one I had the biggest crush on and thought was hot."

"Oh, girl, why do the brothers' best friends have to be so hot? I had the biggest crush on my brother's best friend growing up. Turns out, he was a douchebag, but that didn't stop my sixteen-year-old self from dreaming about him. Thankfully, they aren't still friends, but I remember those days when I lusted after him."

"Sometimes fate has a way of making things work out."

"It sure does," Erin says. "Unless you have any further questions for me, I'll let you get out of here and be in touch as soon as I hear back from the judge."

"I think I'm good. Thanks for everything."

"You're welcome." Erin stands from her seat and

motions for me to go ahead of her. She walks me out to the receptionist's desk. "It was good to see you today. Will I see you at the next home game?"

"Um, I'm not sure. It's Wednesday night, right?"

"Yep," she confirms.

"Weeknights are tough. Jax goes to bed around eight thirty, and I don't ever mess with bedtime when we've got an early morning the next day."

"I get it. I don't make it to all of them, either, so don't feel bad if you can't."

I leave Erin's office feeling cautiously optimistic about the future.

"GO, ZACK!" JAX CHEERS AT THE TV AS WE WATCH the first period of the game. He really enjoys watching the games when we're able to, much like I do. It makes me smile how easily he's taken to Zack. He's so much happier now that we're in Austin and around my family once again.

My phone ringing pulls my attention from the game, and I glance at it to see who is calling. I see Erin's name on the screen, so I grab the phone and head into my bedroom to answer the call.

"Hello," I greet.

"Hi, Courtney, sorry it's so late. I had a dinner meeting tonight and couldn't call earlier."

"No worries. Did you hear back from the courts?" I ask nervously.

"I did, and the judge did as we asked. You've been granted the emergency order. I was also made aware that Mr. Whittle has bonded out of jail. I know you had said he hadn't been in contact recently, but I just wanted you to be aware that he is out. Please be safe and reach out if he tries to contact you directly. If we need to file for a protection order, we can."

"Thank you so much. I'll stay vigilant, but I don't think he'll show up."

"Okay, I'm only a phone call away if you need anything. Have a great night."

I hang up from the call and drop to my bed. I grab my pillow, hugging it to my chest as I let the tears fall. I was so worried the judge wouldn't sign off and I'd have to go through a long-drawn-out battle in the courts. All I want to do at this moment is call Zack and tell him, but I can't since he's on the ice. Instead, I call the next best person.

"Hello," I say when Ryan answers his phone.

"Hey, Sis, everything okay? It sounds like you're crying."

"They are good tears," I tell him as more fall.

"Elaborate more," he says, and I can tell he's on edge.

I word vomit everything to him. Everything I learned the other day at Erin's office. What she just called to tell me.

"Holy shit," he says, probably just as shocked as I was when I first learned about everything going on with Chad. "Makes everything make so much sense now."

"I said the same thing. Do you think I should worry about him showing up now that the judge has ruled in my favor?"

"If he does, I'll kick his ass. Are you worried about him showing up?"

"I wasn't until she put the idea into my head."

"That's a pretty long drive for him to make just to, what, piss off the judge to try to scare you?"

"Just knowing what all he's involved in, I don't want him to try to pull anything stupid that hurts Jax or me."

"Do you want to come stay here for a little while? That way, you aren't alone?"

"That's an idea. Let me think about it tonight, and I'll get back to you tomorrow."

"Okay, if you need anything before then, no matter what time it is, you call me. Understand?" Ryan says.

"Yes, of course. Thank you. I love you."

"Love you, too, Sis. Give that nephew of mine a hug and kiss from me."

"Will do. Talk tomorrow."

> COURTNEY
>
> Can you call me when you're out of the rink? I have some news.

I slip my phone back into my pocket and join Jax out in the living room. The game has gone into the first intermission, so the broadcasters are talking about the game on the TV.

"Are you ready for your shower?"

"Yes," he says, but doesn't attempt to move. He's being kind of fidgety, so my mom spidey senses go on alert.

"Is something wrong or bothering you?"

"When will I see Dad again?" he asks. He hasn't said much about Chad since we left, but I knew he'd eventually ask about him.

I take a seat next to him and mull over what to say. I take his hands in my own. He brings his eyes to mine and stays silent so I can talk.

"I don't know. Your dad loves you. I know that, and you know that," I tell him. I don't ever want to paint Chad in a bad light to Jax. He knows what it was like to be in the same house as him, and he knows what it's been like without him. "I knew when I decided to move here that it would mean not seeing him often, but I had to make what I felt was the best decision to keep us safe and happy. That wasn't something I made lightly. Does that make sense?"

He nods his head, but I don't know if he really understands. "I like it here better, Mommy. I can play and make noise, and he isn't here to get mad." Tears prick my eyes because he's right. No one will be mad at him for being a kid here.

"Exactly, baby. I will do everything in my power to keep it like that."

"I love you, Mommy," Jax says. He pulls his hands from mine and wraps them around me in a big hug. I hold him tightly to my chest and hold back the sobs that threaten to break free from my chest. What I wouldn't do for this boy. I might not be fond of his dad, but I wouldn't change my past for anything because that would mean I wouldn't have Jax.

Once we've had our moment, he jumps down and heads for the bathroom. I get the water turned on and the temperature where he likes it. He takes care of washing himself, only needing me to check and make sure he rinses his hair all the way.

"Fuzzy jammies with feet or ones without feet?" I ask from his bedroom as he's drying off in the bathroom.

"Fuzzy," he calls back. I pull out a pair with clean

underwear and set them out on his bed for him to change into when he gets in.

"Get dressed, and I'll go make us a bedtime snack."

I head to the kitchen and pop a small bag of popcorn to share. He loves this stuff, and the mini bags are the perfect amount for a snack.

Once we've finished our snack, he goes in and brushes his teeth, then picks a book for me to read.

"*Froggy Goes to Camp* again?" I ask.

"Yep!" he confirms.

"I've read this one so many times, you could probably read it from your memory," I tease before opening the book and reading it using the funny voices I've adapted for each character over the hundreds of times we've read these books.

"Good night, Jax. I love you to the moon and back."

"Love you to the moon and back," he replies.

I pull the covers up and tuck him in, pressing a kiss to his forehead. He rolls over onto his side, and his eyes quickly drift closed. I stay still, watching as his little body moves with each breath he takes. He looks so peaceful, and I hope he stays that way. I hope that everything I've done in the past six months is worth it and that he doesn't hate me one day because of it. I eventually turn and put his book back on the shelf before heading out of his room. I stop in the doorway and glance at his sleeping form one last time. "'To the moon," I whisper before closing the door and heading back to the living room. The game is still on TV, and the second period is almost over, at this point. Thankfully, the Fusion has added to their lead.

I jolt awake to the sound of my phone ringing. I must have nodded off on the couch watching the game because when I look at the screen, it is no longer playing, and the name flashing on my phone is Zack.

"Hello," I groggily say, pausing to clear my voice of the sleep.

"Sorry to wake you. Your text said to call. Is everything okay?" Zack asks.

"I must have fallen asleep watching the game. Did you guys win?"

"We did. Seven to three," he confirms.

"Nice."

"What was your text about? What's your news?"

"Erin called. The judge finally signed off on our emergency filing."

"That's fantastic!"

"It is, and I'm so relieved," I tell him, and that's the god's honest truth about that portion of my call with her.

"What's wrong? You don't sound elated about that."

"I am, don't get me wrong. But during our call, she brought up something else, and it just has me on edge."

"What is that?" he asks.

"She let me know that Chad had bonded out of jail. She just wanted me to be aware. We don't have any reason to believe he'd come here and try anything, but she just wanted me on alert. And now that is all I can think of. Jax also asked me about Chad out of the blue tonight, and I had to figure out what exactly to say to him."

"Do you want to come stay at my place? It's secure. I have a state-of-the-art home security system, plus, he'd never think to look for you at my place."

"Ryan offered the same thing when I talked to him. I don't know if that's necessary right now."

"The offer stands if you change your mind. Even if that happens while I'm gone this week, I can give you the garage code to get in with."

"Thank you," I simply say.

"You're welcome. Why don't I let you go so you can get back to sleep and call me tomorrow."

"I can do that."

"Night, Courtney," Zack says.

"Night, Zack," I tell him and end the call.

15

ZACK

I skate down the middle of the ice, the puck on the end of my stick as I skate around a defender, then pass the puck up to Camden. He gains the zone and takes the puck in deep to the corner, where he gets collapsed on by the defense. I drop down to help dig the puck out so we don't lose possession. I get it out and send it around the boards to the other side.

When I turn to skate back to the center, I'm leveled to the ground by a bad hit. The winger from Dallas clipped me on the knee, and I go down quickly and in pain. I roll on the ice, grabbing at my knee as I scream out in pain.

"Fuck," I yell as my teammates kneel next to me. Whitney comes sliding up to me, kneeling to ask me her questions.

"Where's the pain?" she asks.

"On the side of my kneecap," I grit out.

"Is it radiating or staying in one spot?"

"Mostly right there, but it's throbbing, so kind of hard to say specifically," I tell her.

"Okay, sounds like your MCL," Whitney says. "Can you guys help me get him to the bench?" she asks Camden and Easton.

"Yep." They help me up, and with a guy on each side of me, we slowly skate over to the bench. I can't put any weight on my left leg, so I know something is wrong. Whitney follows us, carrying my stick and gloves back to the bench.

The guys help me onto the bench, and then the equipment guys take over, helping me down the tunnel and into the locker room. Whitney follows them and has them help me into the treatment room and onto her exam table.

"I'm going to get some of this gear off you first," she says, and removes the tape on my socks, then removes the sock, along with my shin pad and skate.

"How's it going in here?" A middle-aged man comes in. "I'm Dr. Smith, one of the Dallas team doctors."

"Hi, I'm Whitney, and this is Zack." Whitney introduces both of us.

"Nice to meet you both. What are we dealing with here?" he asks.

"I'm thinking MCL, but I'll let you check him over, and we can go from there," she tells him.

Dr. Smith steps up and starts his exam of my knee. It hurts like a motherfucker, especially when he's poking and prodding at it and asks me to move it. "I agree with your assessment. I'd like to get a quick X-ray, just to rule out any fractures, but I think an MRI will be needed to diagnose you fully. In the meantime, we can get you some pain meds and a brace until you get back home and can get in for the MRI."

"Thanks, Doc," I tell him as Whitney hands me a small cup with some pain meds, along with a water bottle. I pop the meds into my mouth and take a large squirt of water from the bottle, washing down the pills, hoping they'll kick in quick.

I'm helped out of the rest of my gear and then taken down the hall to the X-ray room. One perk of professional sports arenas is they tend to have a lot of medical equipment.

"I don't see any fractures, so at least it isn't broken. I'll get you a knee brace to keep it stabilized and give your team doctor a call to let them know."

"Thank you," Whitney tells him.

"Do you need me to write a script for some stronger pain meds, or do you want to wait for your doctor to do so?"

"I'll be fine," I tell him and hope that's the truth.

Whitney takes me back to the locker room. "Do you want to get showered now?" she asks.

"Probably should. Best to do it now than when it's a madhouse in here," I tell her. She pushes the wheelchair over to my locker, and I grab my shower stuff and some clean clothes to change into. Whitney takes me over to a shower stall, and thankfully, this one has a bench and showerhead on a wand. I transfer over to the bench, and she leaves me to myself.

"Holler if you need any help," she calls out.

I strip from my compression clothes, tossing them out onto the wheelchair. The hot water hits my body, and I start to relax. Being taken out of a game with an injury is never a fun experience. I can only hope that this one doesn't keep me out of the game for long.

By the time the game ends, I'm showered and dressed in a team tracksuit. I'm given a pass on having to wear a suit due to my injury. Once I was showered and dressed, Whitney got the leg brace on me and had me sit with some ice for a while. After that, she fitted me with some crutches so I can get around on my own. While I sat icing my knee, I shot Courtney a text.

ZACK

> I'm guessing you weren't watching the game since I don't have a bunch of texts from you.

COURTNEY

No, was busy with Jax. Why, what's wrong?

ZACK

Had to get carted off the ice by two of the guys. Bad hit to my knee. Nothing is broken, but it's probably my MCL. I'll need an MRI in the next few days.

COURTNEY

Holy shit. Are you sure you're okay? Do you need me to come be your nurse?

ZACK

I mean, if you're offering, I won't pass up having you as my nurse. (winking smile face)

COURTNEY

I knew that was coming. (eye roll) But seriously, how are you?

ZACK

Pain meds have finally kicked in. I'll know more once I have the MRI and know what I'm looking at for recovery. If surgery is required, then my season is over. If I just need some rest and then PT, then it will hopefully only be a few weeks.

COURTNEY

That sucks, I'm sorry.

ZACK

Thanks. How was your day?

COURTNEY

It was fine, nothing major, just another Friday.

ZACK

Still nothing from Chad?

COURTNEY

Nope, still radio silent.

ZACK

Good.

COURTNEY

Do you want me to come over tomorrow? Come take care of you?

ZACK

I'm not going to say no, but if you have other plans, I'll understand.

COURTNEY

Nothing major. I think I'm going to turn in my resignation at the Burger Shack.

ZACK

What made you decide that?

COURTNEY

I'm overwhelmed with working six days a week. While the money is nice, I need the time off more. I also would like not to rely on my brother and parents so much to watch Jax for me. I feel like I'm failing him as a parent with how often he has to be watched by others. I only get so much time with him, and giving up every Saturday is becoming a lot.

ZACK

I think you're a rock star for how hard you work to provide for him. I also think you deserve the time off.

COURTNEY

Thanks. I hope they don't take it too harshly.

ZACK

That isn't for you to worry about. I'm sure by giving them notice, you'll be better than most people who've left as they tend to just stop showing up.

COURTNEY

You're right on that one. I've been working when people didn't show up. Unfortunately, the ones that take the brunt of it are your coworkers who have to fill in and cover for the missing person.

ZACK

I'll probably head to the doctor first thing in the morning, so don't feel like you need to rush over. I'm hopeful they can pull some strings and get me in for the MRI tomorrow.

COURTNEY

Can they do one that fast, or will they need to wait for the swelling to go down?

> ZACK
>
> No clue, to be honest with you. The doctor from Dallas who came in to look me over just mentioned that he'd recommend I have one done to verify his suspicions that it's my MCL.

COURTNEY

Gotcha. Well, keep me posted. I can head over after I pick up Jax from my parents after my shift.

> ZACK
>
> Pack a bag, and you guys can stay the night. Sawyer was going to come over. I'm sure he'll still come, even with my knee the way it is. The boys can help keep each other entertained.

COURTNEY

And let me guess, you'll keep me busy?

> ZACK
>
> Of course!

COURTNEY

Don't tempt me with a good time now.

> ZACK
>
> I can't promise a good time, but I can promise a relaxed time.

COURTNEY

I'm okay with that!

> ZACK
>
> Then it sounds like a date.

ZACK

> Not to cut this short, but the guys are all filing in now that the game is over. I'll text you tomorrow once I know anything.

COURTNEY

> Sounds good. I hope you are able to get some sleep tonight.

ZACK

> Thanks, me too.

I slip my phone back into my pocket as the guys start removing their gear. Coach pops into the locker room and gives his after-game speech. It isn't long, just a little pep talk, letting the guys know how well they played tonight and how important the two points were in the standings.

"You going to live?" Kaden asks once we're loaded on the plane.

"Yeah, just not sure yet how long I'll be out."

"I'm sure Doc will get you all checked out tomorrow."

"That's my hope," I tell him as I try to get comfortable on the plane. I took an entire row to myself, putting up the armrests so I can sit with my leg stretched out. Whitney brings me some pillows to help support my leg, as well as help cushion my back since I'm sitting with my back against the wall of the plane.

"Thanks for the ride," I tell Graham as I carefully

get out of his SUV. I was in no condition to drive myself home, and he offered me a ride.

"No problem, man. Let me know how things are tomorrow or if you need anything in the meantime."

Once inside my house, my knee is throbbing, and I'm exhausted beyond belief. I pop some more pain meds, grab an ice pack from the freezer, and head to bed.

Before we landed, Whitney told me she heard from our team doctor that they'd see me at nine in the morning at his office, so I set an alarm.

"Good morning, Zack," Dr. Jones greets as he enters the exam room.

"Morning, Doc."

"How are you feeling this morning?" he asks.

"Like my knee is fucked up. It is throbbing and pretty swollen."

He unwraps the brace I was given and starts his exam. "To know the extent of the injury, we need an MRI. I'll have one of the techs come and get you, then be back once it's finished, and we can look at the images. Sound like a plan?" he asks.

"Yep," I agree.

"We'll need you to change into this gown and make sure you leave anything metal here in the exam room," he explains before handing me a gown, and then he turns and leaves the room. I change as quickly as I can and only sit here staring at the wall for a couple of minutes before there's a knock on the door and it is being opened again.

"Mr. Blackburn, I'm TJ, and I'll be taking you in for your MRI. Do you want to use your crutches, or would you rather go by wheelchair?"

"How far is it?"

"Down two halls, maybe the length of the sheet of ice away."

"I can go by crutches." I stand and slide the crutches under my arms, and follow TJ down the two halls. When we reach the door marked MRI, he stops us before entering.

"Do you have any metal on you?"

"Just the crutches," I tell him.

"Alright, go ahead and have a seat in this wheelchair. I'll leave the crutches out here in the hallway during the test."

I take a seat in the wheelchair, and he quickly takes me into the room, then helps me transfer onto the table. He gets my leg positioned how he needs me, then takes the wheelchair back out of the room. When he returns, he slips a set of headphones on me, then heads into the control booth.

"Can you hear me okay?" he asks through the headphones.

"Yep," I confirm.

"Good. Only your legs will be in the machine. I'll be taking multiple sets of images; the whole thing should take us maybe twenty minutes. Would you like me to put on some music for you?"

"Uh, sure."

"Any requests?"

"Not super picky, I guess a pop station."

Music starts playing in my ears. "If you want the volume turned up or down, just talk, and I can hear you and adjust it for you. The machine can get kind of loud at times, so don't hesitate to ask."

"Got it."

"Alright, here we go," he says as the bed moves, taking me into the machine. I close my eyes and try to ignore the loud noises the machine makes as it takes the pictures of my knee the doctor needs. "Alright, we're all done," TJ says as the bed moves and I slide out of the machine. It didn't feel like twenty minutes passed, so I'm taking that as a bonus.

TJ helps me back to the exam room and gets me settled on the exam table once again. "Dr. Jones will be in after he reviews the images."

"Thanks," I tell him before he leaves the room.

> **ZACK**
> I just finished my MRI and am waiting for the doctor to come in with the results.

COURTNEY

How are you feeling this morning? I hope it's good news!

> **ZACK**
> Hurts like a bitch and is swollen.

COURTNEY

I'm sorry (frown face emoji)

> **ZACK**
> You can kiss me and make it better (winky face)

COURTNEY

(kissing emoji) Later today.

The door opens, so I toss my phone on top of my clothes on the chair.

"What's the verdict?" I ask Dr. Jones.

"It's a complete tear of your MCL." He doesn't beat around the bush.

"Fuck," I curse, knowing this means my season is over. "Surgery?"

"Because of your job, I'm going to suggest it. Surgery will get you healed faster. We can go in and clean it up, get it stitched back together and you into some PT within a few weeks. Four to six weeks of PT and you should be back on the ice."

"So there's a chance I could make it back during playoffs if we're still in it?"

"I won't make any promises this early, but it is an option on the table, at this point," he says. "I'm going to send a couple of scripts for you. A better anti-inflammatory and a pain med. Just don't drive if you take the pain med."

I'm feeling a little better knowing there's a possibility of returning this season. I just need to focus on my recovery and hope my team doesn't fall apart before I make it back. "Sounds good. When can we schedule surgery?"

"Early in the week. Once you're dressed, we can head to my scheduler's office to get you a date and time."

"Thanks, Doc."

"You're welcome. Sorry about meeting under these conditions, but I'll do my best to get you back out on the ice as soon as possible. Once you're dressed, just open the door, and we'll be ready to show you to Cynthia's office."

"I appreciate it."

He steps out of the room, and I pull the gown off and slip back into my T-shirt, sweats, and knee brace. With the crutches under my arms, I open the door and follow the nurse down the hall and into an office with a middle-aged woman.

"Mr. Blackburn, nice to meet you, big fan," she says as she opens a folder.

"Nice to meet you, ma'am." I might be in pain, but I'm not an asshole.

"I can get you on Dr. Jones's schedule for Tuesday morning. Does that work for you?" she asks.

"Yep, the sooner the better."

"His schedule was filled for Monday, but we've got one last spot for Tuesday, so you're in luck. The hospital will call you on Monday with your check-in time. Plan on it being sometime between six and eight in the morning."

"Okay. Is this just a day surgery, or will I be admitted?"

"Just a day surgery, so you'll need someone to take you home. It's best if they can also stay with you for a few days. You'll be pretty groggy the rest of the surgery day and might need some help getting around for the few after that."

"Not a problem," I tell her. I know my mom will come stay with me, if needed. An idea strikes me, but I'll deal with it once I'm not in the doctor's office on a Saturday morning.

"Alright, I just need a few signatures from you, and then you can get out of here." I sign the papers Cynthia hands me, then return them to her. "This packet is for you to take. It has the information on where you need to go on Tuesday morning. If you haven't received a call with a check-in time by two p.m., give this number a call," she explains, and highlights a phone number on the page.

"Easy enough," I say.

I take the folder she hands me and make my way out to the parking lot. Once I'm settled into my truck, I take a few deep breaths as my knee throbs with all the jostling it's been through this morning.

Before heading home, I stop at the pharmacy, hoping they have my scripts ready. They aren't ready when I pull up, but they tell me they can finish them in ten minutes, so I pull into a spot and wait.

As soon as I get home, I pop the top of the pain med, downing one of the pills to take away this throbbing pain I'm in. I grab an ice pack and head back to bed.

16

COURTNEY

"Zack, honey," I say his name as I run my hand over his cheek. I found him passed out in his bed when I arrived at his house. Thankfully, he gave me the garage code so I could get inside, seeing that he's passed out.

He mumbles something, but I can't make out what he's said, so I lightly shake him once again, repeating myself. "Zack, honey, wake up." That must pull him out of his sleep enough as he opens his eyes, looking around like he doesn't know where he is until his eyes land on mine.

"Sweetheart," he says, and pulls me down onto the bed and into his arms. I'm careful not to hit his leg. I can tell it's swollen, and I'm sure he's in pain. "What time is it?" he groggily asks.

"A little after four," I tell him.

"Damn, the pain meds must have really knocked me out."

"Did they give you something at the doctor's?"

"Yeah, a pain med and an anti-inflammatory so I don't have to pop so many ibuprofens."

"What is the plan?"

"Surgery on Tuesday. PT after that. Depending on how far into the playoffs we go, I might be back for later rounds."

"I'm sorry," I tell him.

"Nothing for you to be sorry about. Just the risks of the job. It wasn't a targeted hit, just a freak accident."

"You're in a much better mood about it than I expected."

"Would you like me to pout? Will it get me more nursing care?" he teases.

"No." I laugh as he tickles my rib cage. I do my best not to squirm and hit his leg. "Stop, I don't want to hurt you," I say.

"Fine," he grumbles at the same time as his stomach also rumbles in protest.

"Are you hungry?"

"Starving. I haven't really eaten since yesterday before the game."

"I can go make you something. What would you like?"

"Not picky. You can order something, if you'd prefer."

"Let me go see what you have, and then I'll decide. I'll be right back."

I quickly head to the kitchen and rummage through the cabinets and fridge. I find some tomato soup and the fixings to make grilled ham and cheese sandwiches.

I make two sandwiches for Zack and one for me, then pour the soup into two bowls. I rummage in the pantry again and find some Ritz crackers to take for the soup. I also find a large tray I can easily put everything on to carry up to the bedroom. Before I leave the kitchen, I grab two bottles of water from the fridge and snag his two prescription bottles off the kitchen island where he left them.

"Do you want to sit up?" I ask as I enter the room. Zack pushes himself up, then adjusts the pillows behind his back.

"I made soup and sandwiches, nothing fancy, but it was quick," I tell him, and set the tray on the bed.

"It smells amazing," he says.

"Do you want me to replace your ice pack?"

"Do you mind?"

"Of course not. Do you need anything else? I brought water and your meds with me, as well," I say as I point at the bottles on the tray.

"You're too good to me." He gives me a sincere smile. I grab the ice pack and run back down to the kitchen. The freezer is stocked with a few reusable ice packs, so I grab a new one and put the warm one back in so it can refreeze.

"Where would you like it?" I ask as I step up to the side of the bed.

"Underneath my knee." Zack lifts his leg up slightly, and I slide the cold pack under his knee. "Shit, that hurts." He sucks in a breath and blows it out slowly as he gets used to the cold pressing on his injury.

I move the tray of food, then join Zack on the bed. I set the tray on his lap, giving him a larger surface for eating.

"Damn, this is good," he mumbles around a bite of sandwich. His bite makes me laugh as it takes at least a quarter of the sandwich.

"I'm a grilled cheese expert. I've made many of them in my days."

"Where's Jax?"

"He's still at my parents'. I called after I got out of work, but they asked if he could stay for a few more hours. They were about to leave for some event at the Children's Museum. Is Sawyer coming over tonight?" I ask.

"I don't really know. I should probably check in with Emerson," he tells me, and reaches for his cell.

He unlocks the screen and scrolls through a ton of notifications. He touches the screen a few times before the ringing of a phone fills the air.

"Hi, Dad!" Sawyer greets when the call connects.

"Hey, buddy, how's it going?"

"Good. Are you okay?" he jumps to the point and asks.

"Not the best. My knee is in bad shape. I have to have surgery on it this week. If you still want to come over tonight, you can. I'm not much for moving around, but you know I always want to see you and spend time with you."

"Mom said it might be best if I wait a few days and let you rest."

"Is that what you want to do?" Zack asks.

"I don't know," he answers quietly, and I can tell he's torn about what he should do.

"I won't be mad with whatever you decide to do. I'm not much company. The pain meds made me sleep all day, so I'll understand if you want to stay at Mom's and come over later in the week. Maybe Mom can bring you by for a little bit while I'm awake?" Zack suggests.

"I'll ask her." Zack's suggestion obviously perks Sawyer up, and it just melts my heart at how, even at this moment of his own pain, he still makes his son a priority. It makes me realize just how much Jax is missing out on a healthy relationship with his dad. "Mom says yes," Sawyer says when he comes back on the line.

"Hey, Zack," Emerson comes over the line.

"Hey, I was asking Sawyer what he wanted to do. I'm not up to doing much, in my state, but I told him if you were able to bring him by for a little bit, I'd be okay with that. He seemed pretty bummed about not coming to see me."

"We're going out for dinner in about an hour. I could drop him off beforehand if you can feed him, and then I can pick him up when we're on our way home, if that works?"

"Yeah, that should be fine. We can order something in," Zack tells Emerson.

"Do you need anything?" she offers.

"I'm good, but thanks for asking. Courtney is here with me, so she's made sure I'm fed and have what I need." My eyes widen at his nonchalant mention of me to his ex.

"So it's serious between the two of you? Sawyer has mentioned her a few times. He's a fan of her son." My heart swells at that.

"I'd like to think that it's serious," he tells her but winks at me. Those damn butterflies take flight in my stomach.

"I'm happy for you, Zack," Emerson tells him, and it makes me tear up at her kindness.

"Thanks. Things are still kind of new, but we're good."

"And Ryan's all good with it?"

"Gave us his blessing, so we're all good on that front, as well."

"Good. I'll drop him off in thirty, maybe forty-five minutes."

"See you then," Zack tells her, and they end the call.

"Do you want to relocate to the living room?" I ask.

"Probably best once he's here, but lie down with me for a few minutes."

I collect our dirty dishes and stack them on the tray, then move that to the dresser for now. I lie back down on the bed next to him and snuggle into his arms. I hum in contentment. "This is quickly becoming one of my favorite places to be."

"Good, get used to it. I'd keep you here forever if I could."

"Don't tempt me with a good time," I tease.

"Woman." He smacks my ass. "I'll chain you to my bed if you're not careful."

I can't stop the giggles from starting, and once they do, it is hard to rein them in.

"What's so funny?" he asks.

"I've just never thought of you as the BDSM type."

"I'm all about the whips and chains, baby," he tries to tell me with a straight face but can't hold it. He ends up laughing right along with me. "Nothing against people who are, but you're right. That just isn't my kink."

"What is your kink, then?" I ask, doing my best to be serious.

"You under me, on top of me, hell, just next to me. I'll take you in any position you want. What about you?"

"I've never really experimented. My kinkiest thing is probably my vibrator."

"Do you get yourself off often?" Zack asks, and I don't miss the fact that he's sliding his hand lower and lower toward my center.

"What do you consider often?" I practically pant as his fingers slip under my leggings and into my panties. He presses his thumb to my clit, and I about fall apart just from that simple touch.

"Do you touch yourself daily? Weekly? Better yet, do you think of me as you slide that vibrator into your pussy?" He slips two fingers inside me as he asks, and I cry out in pleasure.

"Yes," I pant because he's definitely been the star of my dreams and fantasies lately.

"Fuck, you're beautiful when you are like this."

ZACK

Zack nips at my ear, then presses kisses to my throat as his fingers work me over, bringing me right to the edge before he backs off slightly, just to bring me right back to the edge. "Are you ready to come, sweetheart?"

I can't find the ability to say anything. Instead, I let my body do the talking as I come hard on his fingers.

"That's it, beautiful. Give it all to me." My body goes limp on the bed as I bask in my release. Zack slides his hand from my clothes and brings his fingers to his lips, sucking them clean. "I'll never tire of your taste."

"Why is that so hot?" I ask.

"Because it's us, baby. Just us being everything each other needs at the moment."

I sigh in contentment. I'd have never guessed months ago I'd be this comfortable in a relationship. Deep down, I know I've fallen in love with this man, and now I just have to find the right time to tell him.

17

ZACK

Courtney helps me move to the living room and get settled on the couch with my knee all propped up and supported. She's babying me a bit, but I won't complain.

The door opens, and Sawyer and Emerson come walking in. "Hey, Dad!" Sawyer comes running over to the couch and gives me a big hug. I've missed him so much this past week.

"Missed you, buddy," I tell him before letting him go.

"Hi, I'm Courtney." She introduces herself to Emerson.

"Nice to finally put a face to the name." She and Emerson shake hands, and it's so surreal to have these parts of my life finally colliding.

"Sorry for the lack of introduction."

"We won't hold it against you forever. You get a pass because of your condition."

"Thanks, I guess." I roll my eyes at Emerson. She knows I'm just messing with her, just as she's messing with me.

"I gotta run, as we have reservations. It should be a couple of hours, but I can shoot you a text when we're on our way back, if that works?"

"Works for me. How about you, Sawyer?"

"Yep. Bye, Mom." He runs over and gives her a hug goodbye, then shuts the door after she walks out.

"What are you craving for dinner?" Courtney asks him.

"Pizza!" he declares.

"That's easy enough. Do you have a favorite place to order from?" she asks me.

I pull up a pizza place app and hand my phone over so she can put in the order. "Our favorite should be listed in the history, so do that plus whatever you want. When you get to the payment screen, my card should be saved in my account."

Courtney taps at the screen a few times, then hands the phone back to me. "Should be here in about thirty-five minutes," she tells me, then turns to Sawyer. "How're your games going?"

"Good, we keep winning! And I've scored a lot of goals. I'm going to be better than my dad someday." I love his confidence, even if he is a little cocky about it.

"That's awesome. Maybe Jax and I can come watch you play sometime. He loves watching your dad play, so seeing you would be awesome!"

"Sure, maybe Mom can tell you when we play again."

"I have your schedule, as well," I interject.

"I'll take a look at it, and we'll make a plan to come watch you," Courtney says.

We hang out until the pizza is delivered, then gorge on the cheesy, greasy goodness.

Courtney's phone rings, and she answers it. "Hey, yeah, that'd be great," she says to whoever she's talking to before rattling off my address.

"That was my mom and dad. They are done and offered to drop Jax off rather than me having to go get him since they're still out and about."

"That was nice of them."

"They should be here in ten to fifteen minutes."

"Are you staying here?" Sawyer asks.

"Um, I'm not sure. With your dad needing help, I might," she tells him.

"I don't want him to be alone. I was worried," Sawyer says, and my heart melts at my son's kindness.

"That's sweet of you," Courtney says, and Sawyer's cheeks blush at her compliment. He's not usually the gushy type, so I'm glad I got to witness this.

***

THE PAST FEW HOURS ENDED UP BEING JUST WHAT I needed. Some time with my son, and time with Courtney and Jax. The boys kept us well entertained with their jokes and just the random things kids say. The boys feed off one another. I sat back and just soaked in the time together, and it made me realize what life could be like going forward. How we could stitch together our families and make our own pieced-together family.

"I don't want to go to Mom's tonight. I want to stay now," Sawyer says after I tell him that his mom texted saying they were leaving dinner.

"I'm fine with you staying. Do you want me to tell her not to come?"

"Yes."

I call Emerson. "Hey, Sawyer has changed his mind and wants to stay. We're having a great time, so do you mind if he comes back tomorrow?"

"I'm glad that it's been a good time. Tomorrow is perfectly fine. Do you need me to plan on coming to get him?"

"I'll text you tomorrow, and we can work it out."

"Sounds good. Have a good night," Emerson says.

"Mom's good with you staying until tomorrow," I tell him.

"Yes! Can Jax and I have a sleepover in the den?" he asks.

"I don't see why not."

"Where can I find some pillows and blankets for them to set up in there?" Courtney asks.

"There's a chest in there with some, and if needed, we can grab two sleeping bags out of the closet in the garage with all my camping gear."

"You camp?" Courtney asks, her eyebrows pulled up to her hairline in shock.

I chuckle. "Yeah, Sawyer and I go every summer."

"Learn something new every day," she muses.

"There's still a lot to learn about me." I smirk at her, hoping she gets the innuendo.

I know she does when she rolls her eyes.

"Can we turn on a movie in the den?" Sawyer asks.

"*Spider-Man!*" Jax calls out as he follows Sawyer.

"Sounds like a good plan," Courtney tells the boys as she follows them to the den. I grab my crutches and eventually follow them. By the time I make it into the area, Courtney has made makeshift beds on the floor with blankets and pillows.

ZACK

"Why don't you go get ready for bed before we start the movie?" I suggest to Sawyer.

"You do the same, Jax. You can use the stuff in your bag from Grandma's and Grandpa's."

Both boys scamper off and do as asked. I'm not sure how well the teeth brushing goes based on the laughter coming from the bathroom, but at least they're getting along.

"How'd we get so lucky?" Courtney asks as she leans her head on my shoulder. We're sitting side by side on the couch waiting on the boys to return.

"Good parenting usually leads to good kids. We both have both going for us."

"Thank you for everything," she says. "Jax has never been so carefree. I love seeing him so comfortable around you and Sawyer."

"Thank you for sharing him with us," I tell her as the boys come running back into the room. They are both dressed in pj's and have huge smiles on their faces.

"Why do you both look guilty?" Courtney asks.

"We brushed our teeth and got ready, like you said," Sawyer says.

"Alright, giggle butts. Time to get into your blanket forts and get ready for the movie. Then it is bedtime," Courtney instructs. Once the boys settle, she gives them each a hug and kiss on the cheek.

I already have the movie pulled up, ready to hit play once they are settled.

"If you need anything, come get me," Courtney tells both of them.

"Night, Mom," Jax tells her.

"Night, boys," she replies. I make sure the movie is playing before I leave the room. I find Courtney in the kitchen, packing up the few slices of pizza that are left over. Once the food is put away, she starts loading the dishes from earlier into the dishwasher and then moves to wipe down the counters.

"You don't have to clean my house," I finally interject.

"I can't sleep with a dirty kitchen. It has to be cleaned up before I can sleep." She shrugs.

"Are you ready for bed?" I ask once she's finished.

"Yes and no. I feel like I should stay up until they fall asleep, but I also don't know how long that will take. Someone needs to turn off the TV when the movie ends."

"It's on a timer. After a little bit of nothing playing, it will automatically turn off. I purposely had it set up that way."

"That's pretty smart."

"We can go watch our own movie in the living room, then head to bed afterward."

"That's the perfect plan. Can I get you anything? Meds? Ice pack?"

"I'll take both, just the anti-inflammatory for now. The narcotics will knock me out again."

"You get settled on the couch, and I'll be back in just a few minutes."

I do as she says, getting settled on the couch. I pull up one of the many streaming apps I have and start flipping through the options. Courtney returns with my meds, water, and an ice pack. She hands me the meds and water, and I knock the pills back. She then gets the ice pack settled around my knee. The cold instantly chills my body.

"Sit, I need to hold you again," I tell her. She does and snuggles into my side just like I'd hoped she would. *"What do you want to watch?"* I ask.

"Something funny. I'm not in the mood for sad."

I chuckle and hand over the remote. *"You pick, then. I'm good with funny."* She sorts through the romantic comedy section, finally picking *How to Lose a Guy in 10 Days*.

"This okay?" she asks as the opening credits start.

"Yep," I tell her. I don't know if I've ever watched this one from start to finish, and if I have, it's been years, seeing as the movie is from the early 2000s.

Once the movie ends, I turn the TV off. Courtney fell asleep on my shoulder, and I don't want to move her, but nature calls, so I need to get up. Also, sleeping like this all night will give her one kinked neck come morning.

"Court, sweetheart, wake up," I whisper as I shift to cup her face.

She stirs, then bolts upright, stretching her neck as she does.

"Sorry for falling asleep."

"You can use my shoulder as a pillow anytime," I tell her before pressing my lips to hers. "I need to go to the bathroom, then bed."

"I'll go check on the boys, then meet you in the bedroom."

"I look forward to it." I wink before we both stand. She waits to make sure I have my feet under me with the crutches before she takes the warm ice pack back to the kitchen. I make my way to the bedroom, then the bathroom as quickly as I can.

When I come out of the bathroom, Courtney is standing next to the bed, pulling one of my T-shirts on over her naked body. My own body instantly responds to seeing her standing there like that's her side of the bed and where she belongs. Naked is even better.

"You could just leave that off. I wouldn't complain," I tell her as I come over to the bed.

"Nice try. Not with kids that could need me at any moment of the night."

I slip a hand up the shirt, cupping one of her breasts. My thumb grazes over her nipple, the peak already hard and giving away her arousal.

"I can't get enough of you," I say as I lay her back on the bed and kiss her. I deepen the kiss, needing to show her just how much I need her, how much she means to me, and how much I love her. I pull back when that thought hits me. I love this woman.

"What's wrong?" she asks, worry written all over her beautiful face.

"Nothing, nothing at all. I just have this inexplicable need to make sure you know just how much you mean to me, how you've changed my life for the better, and most importantly, I need you to know that I'm head over heels in love with you."

"I love you, too," Courtney whispers.

My lips crash back against hers. If it weren't for this fucking knee injury, we wouldn't be getting any sleep tonight.

18

COURTNEY

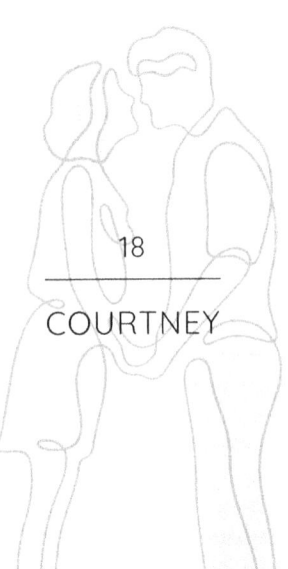

THE PAST TWO MONTHS HAVE BEEN LIKE A whirlwind. Zack had his surgery and was able to start PT almost immediately after. He's been kicking ass working hard to get back to his fully healthy self. The Fusion made the playoffs and are still on the chase for the Cup. Today is the first day he's going to practice with the team. He'll be wearing a red jersey, which means he's no-contact by the other guys, but at least it's a step in the right direction.

I keep checking my phone whenever I have a second while at work, hoping he'll text me to let me know how practice goes. He was ready and nervous for it, all at the same time, this morning. It was extremely cute seeing him with those mixed emotions. Like a little boy again.

With him recovering and needing help so much,

ZACK

Jax and I have been staying at his place more than we have at my apartment. I love the nights I get to be in Zack's arms, but I also struggle with it being too soon for us to be moving in with him for good.

> ZACK
>
> Hey, sweetheart. Hope your day is going good. Practice was great! It felt good to be back out there with the guys. No pain after getting off the ice either, so I think I'm back!
>
> COURTNEY
>
> That's the best news! I'm so proud of the work you've put in. You deserve it.
>
> ZACK
>
> Can I have you as a reward tonight?
>
> COURTNEY
>
> Yes
>
> ZACK
>
> I'm going to have you moaning my name so much. Fuck, I'm already hard thinking about it.
>
> COURTNEY
>
> You're incorrigible.
>
> ZACK
>
> Only about you. Gotta go, love you.
>
> COURTNEY
>
> Love you too. See you after work.

SAMANTHA LIND

ZACK
I'll take care of dinner.

I tuck my phone back in my pocket and pick up the toddler at my feet asking to be picked up. He's a sweet little thing who loves to be rocked, so I appease him by swaying with him for a few minutes. He lays his sweet little head on my shoulder as we move back and forth. I can feel his breathing slow down as he relaxes into my hold.

"He's out," my coworker Melanie says as she looks over at us.

"I figured so. His mom said he's been cutting some new teeth, and it's been messing with his sleep. Poor guy probably isn't feeling the best."

I slowly get up, hoping I don't wake him with my movements. I'm somehow able to transfer him to one of the nap cots without waking him up. I cover him with one of our small blankets and hope his little nap helps him feel better.

"Mom, Mom, Mom." Jax is brimming with excitement when I get to Zack's house. He's been picking him up from school for me so he doesn't have to stay so late in the after-school care program.

"What, buddy?" I ask as I set my stuff down. He's jumping up and down he's so excited.

"School has a LEGO club starting. Can I do it, please, please, please?"

"That sounds like fun. Did they send anything home on it?" I ask, and he thrusts a piece of paper into my hands.

I laugh at how excited he is. I take the paper and read it over. It's after school on Tuesdays and Thursdays for six weeks, starting next week. "I can get you signed up for it tonight. It sounds like it will be a good time," I tell him, and he wraps me in a big hug.

"Thank you, Mommy," he says. "Zack also said I can start learning to skate in a few weeks!"

"He did, huh?" I look over at him, my eyebrow popped in a questioning manner.

"New flyers were posted at the rink today with the next set of lessons. Registration is open now, so if it works out with your schedule, he can get started."

"Did it say when they are?" I ask. Jax runs off, leaving Zack and I alone in the kitchen. He quickly closes the distance between us and pulls me into his arms.

"There were multiple options. Weekday evenings and a couple of weekend options, as well."

"I don't know if I could do a weeknight option, so I'll have to check out the weekend ones. I still can't believe you've convinced him to try ice-skating." I lean in and kiss him.

"What can I say? I'm a convincing guy." He smirks. "Now, if only I can convince his mom to do something..." He doesn't finish the sentence, leaving me wondering what he wants to convince me to do now.

We're interrupted when both the boys come running into the kitchen. "When is dinner?" Sawyer asks. "I'm starving."

Zack looks behind him at the timer on the oven. "Food should be on the table in less than fifteen minutes. The timer has just over ten, so not much longer," he tells both boys.

They take off, leaving the two of us alone yet again. "What do you think you need to convince me of?" I ask, not wanting to miss out on what he's thinking.

Zack cups my cheeks with his hands, the way they cradle me and make me feel secure and protected is still surreal to me. "Move in with me. Let's stop this back-and-forth craziness. You're here most nights anyway, so why keep paying for your apartment and all the utilities? You could put that money into savings."

"You're really ready for that step?" I ask.

"I am, are you? I know you worked your ass off to provide a safe place for you and Jax, and I don't want to take that away from you, but the way I see things, I don't want to be away from you more than I have to, and this just feels natural. You coming home from work, the boys running around together when Sawyer is here, family dinner, movie nights. Maybe one day we add another one or two," he says.

"You want more kids?" I ask, shocked at that. I'd never broached the topic with him as I didn't think it was something he was interested in. I've always been on the fence about wanting more kids.

"With the right person, yes."

"And I'm the right person?" I smile up at him.

"The only person." He presses a kiss to my lips, and we only break apart when the timer on the stove goes off.

"I love you," I tell him before we pull apart. He goes to the oven and pulls out the food while I pull out the plates and silverware to set the table. I grab the side dishes he's made and help get everything to the table. "Boys, dinner is ready," I call out loud so they can hear me where they're playing video games in the den.

I soak in the time as we all sit around the table for dinner. This has become normal over the past couple of months, and I can see what Zack was talking about. How could I give this up? As scary as it is, I know that this is the next natural step in our relationship. There's no sense in fighting it.

With the boys tucked into bed and the kitchen cleaned up from dinner, I can finally relax and feel good about going to bed. I find Zack packing his suitcase for the road trip. The team is headed out tomorrow for the next set of games. He won't be playing but will be going to support his teammates and to keep practicing with the team.

"Hi, beautiful," he greets as I enter the bedroom. I close the door behind me and watch as his eyes flare with desire.

"Hi," I greet. "You all packed?"

"For the most part. Just need to toss in a few things in the morning." He closes the distance between where he stands by the bed and where I'm still standing by the bedroom door.

He reaches out and grabs my wrists, pulling both of my hands up and over my head. He holds both wrists in one of his hands and pins them to the wall. My breaths are coming fast as I anticipate his next move. "Should I tease you all night?" He smirks as his lips come to my neck. He tortures me in the best way possible, teasing his lips along all the sensitive spots he knows drives me nuts. The scruff that has grown out on his cheeks with them being in the playoffs is like my kryptonite lately. Just one rub of that against any of the tender spots on my body, and I'm ready for more.

"No, I can't take the teasing that long," I tell him as

I attempt to rub my body against his for some much-needed friction.

"How quiet can you be?" he asks, pressing another kiss to my neck.

"That depends. What are you going to do to me?" I volley back.

"Make you delirious with pleasure," he tells me.

He drops to his knees, and I worry that he'll hurt his knee, but he doesn't even flinch. He pops the button of my jeans, then lowers the zipper. The pink lace on my panties is exposed, and he leans forward, pressing his lips to the spot just above where my panties sit. He slips his fingers inside the waistband of my jeans and tugs them down, leaving my panties in place. He brings the jeans down to my feet, then helps me step out of each leg. They get tossed out of the way once I've done so.

Zack rubs his thumb along my seam. The friction from the thin layer of cotton between us drives me crazy. "I need more," I moan as he teases me.

"Like this?" He looks up at me as he slips a finger under the fabric, pulling my panties to the side and exposing my center to him. His thumb brushes over my clit, and my hips involuntarily move forward, seeking more from him.

"Yes, but more," I tell him.

"Greedy girl." He chuckles before latching his lips

around my clit. I slide my fingers into his hair, holding him to me as he devours me.

Zack pulls back, quickly tugging my panties off my body and out of his way. He lifts my left leg and places it over his shoulder, opening me up to him even more. He dives right back in, his fingers sinking into me as his mouth latches back onto my clit. It doesn't take much for him to have me sailing over the cliff and calling out his name. I cover my mouth as best as I can to muffle the sounds. Thankfully, the boys' rooms aren't down this hall, so we have some distance that will help buffer the sounds.

"That was number one for tonight." He smirks up at me after pulling back.

"Number one?" I ask. "Just how many do you think you can give me tonight?"

"Don't challenge me, woman." He stands and takes me with him, tossing me over his shoulder before depositing me on the bed. He pushes my legs apart and settles between them as he hovers over my half-naked body. "I'll have you coming all night if you let me."

We both strip, not wanting any clothing in our way. I lose track of the number of positions we end up in before we're both so exhausted and satisfied. I eventually pull myself out of bed and go clean up in the bathroom, then pull on some panties and a T-shirt to fall asleep in. Once we're both back in bed, Zack pulls me into his arms, and I'm in my absolute favorite place once again. "The answer to your question is yes," I say into the quiet room.

"I knew I could convince you," he confidently says.

"Is that what tonight was all about?" I laugh.

"Maybe." He smiles and kisses the top of my head. "We can move all of your stuff here when I'm back. I'm sure I can convince Ryan to help with his truck if I promise a nice steak dinner after we're done."

"Probably."

"Love you," he tells me.

"Love you," I tell him just as I drift off to sleep.

19

ZACK

ONE YEAR LATER

I sit out on the deck of our vacation rental, looking out on the water as the sun rises. It's early, and everyone else is still asleep. I couldn't sleep, so I slipped out here as quietly as I could, not wanting to wake anyone.

I sip a cup of coffee as I watch the sky change color, getting brighter and brighter as the sun rises over the horizon. Life's been crazy the past year. I fully recovered from my injury but missed getting to play again when we were eliminated from the playoffs. Had we made it to the next series, I'd have been cleared, but that just made me even more determined to come back the next season. We played our asses off but fell short once again, this time in the conference finals. We were one step away from making the finals, but it just wasn't in the cards for us this season.

"Mornin'," Ryan says as he comes out on the deck and joins me. He blows on the cup of coffee in his hand.

"Mornin'." I give him a head lift in greeting. "What has you up so early?"

"The good ole internal alarm clock." He chuckles. *"It's a bitch when on vacation. What's the plan for today?"*

I look behind us to make sure no one else is awake and coming out to join us. "Lazy morning, then Allison will be taking Courtney to the spa for their pampering day. She did a great job convincing her they should go this afternoon before we go out to dinner," I tell him. It was all part of my plan to spoil her before tonight. "I have things all planned out. A photographer is booked to capture the entire thing on camera. The company I booked to set up the proposal on the beach will be here once the girls are gone, so she won't see anything until she gets back. Then, as the sun sets, I'll drop to one knee." I go over the plans with him.

"Sounds like the perfect plan. Happy for you, brother. Thanks for making my sister so happy."

"I'm the lucky one," I tell him and truly feel that way.

"Morning," Courtney greets us as she joins us. *"You two are up early."* I pat my lap for her to come sit on. She comes over and curls up with me on the lounge

chair. I push her hair out of the way and press a kiss to her temple.

"Morning, baby. Did you sleep well?"

"Yes, until I woke up and you were gone."

Ryan groans from his seat. "My eyes," he complains, but we all know he's just giving us shit and doesn't really mean it.

"Zip it," Courtney tells him. "You are the same way with Allison, so you've got no room to talk."

"But she isn't Zack's sister." He chuckles.

"Potato, potahto," she says, and I just know she's rolling her eyes at him.

"Now, now, children. Do I need to send you both to your rooms?"

"Only if you come with me," Courtney whispers into my ear. My cock swells at the thought of taking her back to bed, but not with everyone waking up. That will have to wait until tonight when I can make love to her for the first time as my fiancée.

"Mom, can we have breakfast?" Jax sticks his head out the door and asks.

"Yep," she tells him and hops off my lap. Ryan and I stay outside for a little while longer, only heading inside when the smells from breakfast start to waft out to us.

"Damn, sweetheart," I say to Courtney when I find her in the kitchen. She's flipping pancakes and has a plate filled with sausage, bacon, and hash browns. It's a full feast this morning. "I didn't realize you were going all out today."

"Just felt like something more than bagels or cereal." She gives me a quick kiss before turning back to the stove and flipping the pancakes. I grab a plate and fill it with the potatoes, sausage, and a couple of strips of bacon. I wait until the kids have each gotten a few pancakes before I take a few and head back outside to eat. Once she's done cooking, Courtney joins me out on the deck. The sun is fully up now, as is everyone in the house.

"What's the plan for today?" I ask.

"I think just hang out on the beach until Allison and I head out. The bigger question is, what are you boys going to do while the women are gone?" she asks.

"I'm sure we can find some kind of trouble to get into," Ryan says.

"Why doesn't that surprise me?" she asks.

"I was thinking of maybe renting some Jet Skis and going out in the water for a few hours," I tell her. That's what we're doing tomorrow. She just doesn't know it.

"That sounds like fun. I'm sure the boys will be ecstatic."

We hang out for the next few hours. The boys take a football down to the beach, and we all toss it around, which ends in a game of tag on the sand. Today is turning out to be the best day, and I can't wait for the rest of it to unfold.

"Okay, girls are gone, let's get to work!" I say to everyone.

"When will the rental company be here?" Ryan asks just as the doorbell rings. "Guess that answers that."

I head for the front door and greet the company here to set up everything for my romantic proposal on the beach tonight.

While they are setting up the arch that is draped with flowers with a neon sign that hangs in the center that reads *Will You Marry Me?*, the boys help me by putting out the solar lights to make a walkway from the back deck to the archway. I want it perfect, and they do a great job placing them every foot or so, creating a walkway between the two areas. "Looks great!" I tell them.

In front of the arch, they place a blanket and spread out a bunch of battery-operated candles to help light the area after the sun sets. The plan is for me to text Ryan when we finish with dinner, and they will

ZACK

make sure everything is turned on and ready for when we get back.

Once I'm satisfied that everything is perfect, I head inside to get dressed for the night out. I grab Courtney's outfit and take it with me to the salon that her and Allison are at. She's a little confused when I show up, but I convince her to come with me. I take her to another salon that does her hair and makeup, then allows her to get changed in one of their private treatment rooms.

When she walks out of the room, dressed, with her hair and makeup perfect, she steals my breath away. "Come here, beautiful," I say as I hold my hand out for her to take. She links her fingers with mine as I pull her into me.

"I feel like a princess," she says before I kiss her. I don't want to mess up her makeup, so I don't deepen it like my body screams at me to do.

"I hope you feel like a queen by the end of the night. My queen," I tell her before whisking her away to the fancy steakhouse I got us reservations at.

"This has all been so much today," Courtney says once we're seated at the restaurant.

"I wanted it to be special and for you to feel pampered," I tell her.

"Well, you've accomplished your goal. It's been one of the best days ever."

If she only knew what was to come.

Dinner was amazing, even if I didn't really taste much of the food. I just wanted to get us back to the beach house and Courtney down to the water so I could pop the question.

We pull into the driveway, and I shut off the engine. "Will you take a walk with me down by the water? We can watch the sunset."

"Of course," Courtney agrees. I lean over the center console and press a kiss to her lips.

"Stay there. I'll come get your door."

I hop out of the rental and go around to the passenger side, opening the door, then assisting Courtney out of her seat. I had the fleeting thought to blindfold her, but I decided against it due to the steps down to the beach.

We walk side by side, fingers linked together as I lead us around the side of the house and down the steps. Courtney leans her head against my shoulder as we walk. "This is probably the most romantic date we've had," she muses. She'll soon find out just how romantic it will end.

We round the back of the house, and the gasp that leaves her tells me she sees what we've set up.

"Don't cry, beautiful," I tell her as I take her cheeks in my hands. I press a chaste kiss to her lips, then pull back. "Come with me?" I ask.

"I'd go with you anywhere." She smiles up at me, tears brimming along her lashes. I lead her to the pathway that is all lit up with the lights. The battery-operated candles have all been turned on, as has the lit sign in the archway. "I can't believe you did all this," she says and looks around.

We make it to the archway, and I turn us so we're facing one another. I take her hands in mine, giving them a little squeeze as I suck in a deep breath and center myself so I don't fuck this up.

"Courtney." I say her name, then have to pause so I can clear my throat before continuing. "We've known each other for the majority of our lives. Little did I realize all those years ago you'd be the one I couldn't wait to come home to. The one I was meant to spoil and make my queen. You've brought so much love to my life. The way you stepped in when I needed you the most, the way you let me be the support you needed in your times of need showed me the man I need to be for you. You are the last thought in my mind before I fall asleep at night and the first thought when I wake up each morning. You are the one I want to go to first with the good and bad. You are my person, my love," I tell her as tears stream down her face.

I reach into my pocket and pull out the ring box I slipped into it when I got out of the car before coming down to the beach. I drop to one knee and open the ring box.

"Courtney Nicole Stevens, will you marry me?" I ask, and tears threaten to fall from my own eyes as I wait for her answer.

"Yes!" she cries out as her arms wrap around my neck. I wrap her up in my arms, standing and taking her with me. "I love you so much," she tells me before crashing her lips to mine.

"I love you, too, my queen." I set her back on her feet so I can take the ring out of the box and slip it on her finger. "Perfect fit," I say before kissing her fingers.

We hear cheering coming from the balcony of the house and turn to find Ryan, Allison, Jax, and Sawyer all up there cheering for us. "Look over there, baby," I whisper into her ear, pointing out the photographer.

"You got it all on camera?" she asks, astonished.

"Not only pictures, but video, as well."

"You really did think of everything," she says before kissing me again.

"You can thank Allison for the video and professional photographer. I was just going to ask her to take pictures, but she said a pro should do it. She did the research and found people for me."

"Thank you. This was more than I could have ever dreamed of in a proposal. You've set the bar high, fiancé."

"When can I make you my wife?" I quirk a brow.

Courtney laughs. "Can we enjoy being engaged for a little bit? I need to get used to it for at least a day or two before I even start thinking about setting a date. But I promise I won't make you wait long. I can't wait to be your wife."

"Before the end of the year?" I ask, hopeful.

"No promises, but we can look at the calendar once we're back home."

The photographer comes over, out of where she's been hidden from view. "How about a few posed pictures?" she asks. "I'm Caitlin, by the way. It's so nice to meet you."

"Yes, please. And nice to meet you. Thank you for being here today," Courtney tells her.

"My pleasure. Now, can I get the two of you facing one another, put your foreheads together and look into one another's eyes, then bring your hands out to show off that amazing ring."

We do as Caitlin says, moving from pose to pose as she gets all the shots.

"Alright, you two, I think I've gotten all the poses I

can think of with just the two of you. Did you want any with the boys?"

"I'd love that!" Courtney tells her.

"I didn't even think to have them get dressed nicely," I tell her.

"That doesn't matter to me. I just want a nice family photo to put on the mantel."

"Hey, boys," I call up to the house, "you're wanted down here."

When they come down, they are dressed in coordinating short-sleeve button-up shirts and shorts.

"I figured you guys would want some family pictures, so I made sure the boys coordinated," Allison says.

"You really thought of everything. Thank you so much!" Courtney says, pulling Allison into a hug.

We get more pictures with the boys, some of just Courtney with Jax, and me with Sawyer. Once done, it is finally time to pop open the champagne and celebrate our forever.

20

COURTNEY
THREE MONTHS LATER

I STAND AT THE BATHROOM SINK. THE TEST THAT will change our lives forever sits in front of me as the hourglass on the screen blinks. The next three minutes will probably be the longest three of my life.

After our engagement three months ago, we decided not to really try but also not prevent getting pregnant, so when I started feeling a little off this week, I figured it was a good time to take a test. Today also happens to be our wedding day. A surprise wedding for our family and friends. We had to tell Ryan and Allison a week ago, as we asked Ryan to officiate and needed to have him get licensed to do so. They were over the moon excited for the two of us and have kept their lips sealed about our plans.

After returning from the beach, we sat down to figure out when we wanted to have our wedding. It is almost impossible to have one during the season, and Zack didn't want to wait until the next offseason, so we came up with the idea to have a backyard wedding just before the season started.

I've spent the last ten weeks planning everything. From the tent for the backyard, to the food, drink, our outfits, and first dance song. All of it has been my focus. We surprised the boys last night and told them, asking them to help us pull off the surprise today for everyone.

The test screen finally stops flashing at me, changing from the hourglass to the word I've been waiting for.

I leave the bathroom with a million things to do before people start to arrive in seven hours. Everyone invited thinks they are coming for an engagement party that we waited to have until the guys were back from camp before the season started.

"Hello, my beautiful bride," Zack greets me as he enters the kitchen. His hand slides around my waist, settling on my abdomen. "I can't wait to slide into you tonight as my wife," he whispers before nipping at my ear.

"Good morning." I turn in his arms and bring my own up and around his neck. "Patience, my future husband."

"What do you need me to do this morning?"

"Just be here to let the rental company in the backyard. They should already have the layout of where to set everything up. The food truck will be here at two. The florist is coming at ten and the baker around two. I should be back around noon with hair and makeup done to get dressed in my pre-ceremony outfit."

"I can't believe we're pulling it off."

"It will be a miracle, but no matter how it goes, as long as I'm yours at the end of the night, that's all I care about."

"Love you." He leans in and kisses me.

"Love you, too. I have to go so I'm not late."

"Drive safe," he says as I grab my keys and purse and head out the door.

EVERYONE IS HERE AND MINGLING. THEY STILL don't realize that we'll be getting married in just a few minutes. The time has come for me to get changed, so I give Ryan and then Zack the signal they are expecting. I sneak away to go back up to our room to change into my dress. Ten minutes later, I hear Zack enter the bedroom to change into his suit that is laid out on the bed. I'm hidden away in the walk-in closet so he doesn't see me until I walk out downstairs.

Once Zack returns, he and Ryan will ask all of our guests to turn their attention to the back door of the house and I'll appear, in my wedding dress, walking toward my future.

Zack

I stand at the closet door; Courtney is just on the other side of it, dressed and ready to become my wife. "Are you ready, sweetheart?"

"More than anything," she says confidently.

I crack the door open, only enough to reach my hand in. She links our fingers together, and I give them a little squeeze.

"I love you. See you in just a couple of minutes, wife."

"Sounds good, husband." One last squeeze of our fingers and I pull away and leave the bedroom. I take in a few deep breaths before I descend the steps and back into the party.

"Damn, man, why are you looking so sharp?" Graham asks. "Oh shit." He brings his fist to his mouth. "This isn't a damn engagement party. This is your wedding day," he states loudly, which gets the attention

ZACK

of a lot of the guests. A hush comes over the group, and that's my moment to shine.

"Hello, everyone, and thank you for coming. I'd like to ask everyone to gather outside under the tent, then turn your attention to the back door of the house where my bride-to-be will be making her exit. Thank you."

The murmurs that quickly spread throughout the crowd have everyone moving to the tent outside. I walk up to the front, where we've decorated to be where we'll stand and exchange our vows. Ryan follows me up there, taking his place as the officiant.

I wait what feels like forever for the back doors to open and for Courtney to emerge. She's drop-dead gorgeous in her white gown. It takes my breath away seeing her walking the short distance to me. The way she glows as she walks with Jax by her side. He escorts her to the front, then gives me a fist bump before joining Sawyer not far from us.

"I love you," I mouth to Courtney as she stands facing me. We link our hands together as Ryan starts the ceremony. We decided to go with a very simple and basic ceremony with the standard vows. With all the other planning we did on such short notice, we decided this was the easiest way.

"By the power vested in me by the state of Texas, I now pronounce you husband and wife. Zack, you may kiss your bride," Ryan says, and I don't hesitate. One hand goes behind Courtney's neck to support it and the other behind her back as I lay my lips to hers and kiss while dipping her back.

The crowd cheers loudly as we continue to kiss, and I'm pretty sure I hear one of my teammates yell at me to get a room.

When we break apart and turn to face everyone, Ryan pipes back up. "I'd like to introduce to you for the first time, Mr. and Mrs. Zack Blackburn."

We walk down the makeshift aisle to the congratulations of our friends and family.

"I think we successfully pulled that off," I tell Courtney when we're back inside.

"I think so. When did everyone figure it out?" she asks as we hold one another and have a moment to ourselves.

"Graham figured it out when I walked out in my suit. He made one comment, and that got a lot of people's attention, so I used that moment to ask everyone to head to the tent," I tell her.

"You're married!" Allison exclaims as she comes around the corner and finds us.

"We are!" Courtney exclaims. "Thank you again for your help this week."

"Of course. I just can't believe you did it so quickly. It feels like just yesterday when we were making all the plans for Zack to pop the big question."

"Speaking of popping the big question, when is my brother going to get off his butt and ask you?"

"You'll have to ask him that," Allison says as she looks around for Ryan.

"I'll start giving him more nudges and hints," Courtney tells her.

"It will happen when it happens. No rush," Allison states.

We're quickly swept up by everyone wanting to congratulate us and shocked that we were able to trick them with such an important event. It was everything we wanted.

Courtney

"May I have this dance, wife?" Zack asks as the music flows. The day and night have been amazing. My dream wedding come to fruition. I wouldn't have changed anything about today.

"Of course," I tell him as I slip my hand into his. He leads me out onto the dance floor, spinning me out and then into his arms. I bring my arms up and behind his neck, then look up into his eyes. I see them filled with so much love and devotion. "Thank you for today."

"I'm the one that should be thanking you," he replies.

There are only a few other couples out on the dance floor with us. The crowd has started to thin out as the hours have ticked by today. The music is just loud enough to drown out the chatter from those talking, whether on the dance floor or just in the backyard.

"I have a wedding present for you," I whisper into Zack's ear.

"You are my present, and I plan to unwrap you very soon. We just need to kick everyone out first."

My head tips back as I laugh at him. I knew that kind of response was coming. "That isn't my gift."

"What more could you top off this day with?" he asks.

I lean up on my tiptoes, bringing my lips to his ear so only he can hear me. "We're pregnant. We're going to have a baby."

"Are you serious?" Zack pulls me back, looking me in the eyes.

"Yes." I nod, tears already threatening to spill from my eyes.

"Fuck yes." He sighs as his lips crash to mine. "How long have you known?" he asks once he pulls back.

"I took a test this morning, so only today," I tell him.

"I can't believe you held it in that long."

"I wanted to surprise you."

"Well, you accomplished that." He tugs me in for a hug and buries his face in my neck. "I love you so damn much, both of you. And the boys, too."

I chuckle at how he keeps adding people to that statement.

"We're going to have one big, happy, blended family," I tell him.

"I can't wait. Sounds like the perfect life to me."

Want to see where Courtney and Zack are nine months later? Download their bonus scene now!

Ready to head back to Austin? Graham and Savannah are up next in Graham.

COMING SOON

To find out what's next from Samantha, please visit her website at samanthalind.com

ALSO BY SAMANTHA LIND

INDIANAPOLIS EAGLES SERIES

Just Say Yes ∼ Scoring The Player

Playing For Keeps ∼ Protecting Her Heart

Against The Boards ∼ The First Intermission

The Hardest Shot ∼ The Game Changer

Rookie Move ∼ The Final Period

Box Set 1 {Books 1-3} ∼ Box Set 2 {Books 4-6}

Box Set 3 {Books 7-10}

INDIANAPOLIS LIGHTNING SERIES

The Perfect Pitch ∼ The Curve Ball

The Screw Ball ∼ The Change Up

LYRICS & LOVE SERIES

Marry Me ∼ Drunk Girl

Rumor Going 'Round ∼ Just A Kiss

STANDALONE TITLES

Tempting Tessa

Then You Came Along

When I Found You

Cocky Doc

Sweet Valley, Tennessee

Nothing Bundt Love

Nothing Bundt Forever

San Francisco Shockwaves

Ryker ~ Aiden ~ Tristan

Damien ~ Blake

Austin Fusion

Zack

ACKNOWLEDGMENTS

Seven years ago when I started on this journey, I never thought I'd be where I am today. Seven years ago I jumped off the edge head first into writing stories that I hope you have come to love. In that time, I've written over 1.6 million words, across 30 novels! I've been part of projects like the Dissent anthology that raised over a half of a million dollars for a very important cause, and made such an impact. I became a *USA Today* Bestselling author, checking off one of the many milestones I never thought I'd reach. And that is ALL thanks to you, my amazing readers! To everyone who has supported me, thank you! Thank You for the impact you have made on my life and my writing. Please know that I appreciate you all!

xoxo,

Samantha

ABOUT THE AUTHOR

Samantha Lind is a *USA TODAY* Bestselling contemporary romance author. When she's not dreaming up new stories, she can often be found with her family, traveling, reading, watching her boys on the ice or watching her favorite professional team (Go Knights Go!).

Connect with Samantha in the following places:

www.samanthalind.com
samantha@samanthalind.com

Reader Group
Samantha Lind's Alpha Loving Ladies
Good Reads
https://goo.gl/t3R9Vm
Newsletter
https://bit.ly/FDSLNL

facebook.com/SamanthaLindAuthor

x.com/samanthalind1

instagram.com/samanthalindauthor

bookbub.com/authors/samantha-lind

Printed in Great Britain
by Amazon